THE CHALET
SCHOOL IN EXILE

ELINOR M. BRENT-DYER

Armada

CONTENTS

CHAPTER I

CHANGES COMING

'YOU look painfully worried, Jem. What's gone wrong now?'

Doctor Jem Russell, head of the Sonnalpe Sanatorium in Tyrol, glanced at his young sister-in-law, Jo Bettany, with a worried air indeed, but he shook his head at her question, and refused to give her a definite answer, much to her suppressed wrath.

'There are a good many things to worry me, Jo. Don't bother me now, that's a good girl. Instead, suppose you go and get some of the ink off your fingers? Have you been bathing in it by any chance?'

Jo regarded her stained fingers ruefully. 'I don't know where it all comes from. That wretched pen of mine doesn't *seem* to leak, and yet I always get into a mess like this when I've been really busy.'

'Perhaps,' suggested the doctor, who knew her, 'you've been dipping it into the ink instead of taking the trouble of filling it properly.'

Jo went pink. 'I *did* think it a waste of time when I was in the middle of my new chapter,' she acknowledged with engaging frankness.

'Well, now you've got to waste your time washing your hands and using pumice-stone into the bargain. I don't see what you gain by it.'

'Doesn't matter now. I've finished the chapter, and I'm stuck.'

'Well, go and clean up, then. Oh, and tell me where Madge is, please?'

'In the nursery, telling stories to the babies—or she was when I came down. Shall I tell her you want her as I go past?'

'No; don't bother. I'll go up to her there. You trot along.'

Jo gave him an impish grin, and turned and ran up the stairs along the wide corridor to the bathroom, where she found her adopted sister, Marya Cecilia Humphries, commonly known as Robin, very busy washing gloves.

'Do you want the basin, Joey?' she asked, moving to one side as she spoke.

'No, thanks. I'll wash under the bath-tap.' And Jo suited the action to the word.

Robin went on with her work, only pausing when an impatient exclamation from Jo drew her attention. 'What is it, then, Jo?' she asked, with the pretty turn of speech that reminded people that in her early years she had spoken mainly French. 'Is the water too hot?'

'No,' said Jo, 'but I can't get this ink off my hands. I don't believe they'll ever be clean again!'

'You have said that before. Try methylated spirit. Corney Flower got walnut-juice stains off her fingers with it, so it ought to be as good for ink.'

'I can *try*,' said Jo dubiously, tossing down the nail-brush with which she had been scrubbing her fingers in the hope of getting them clean again. 'Where shall I find any?'

'Try Madge's cupboard. She has some there, I think.'

Jo departed to seek the spirit, and the Robin, having squeezed as much water from her gloves as possible, wrapped them in a towel, patted them thoroughly, and then laid the bundle into the big airing-cupboard to dry, before she rinsed her hands and dried them, and went off to the nursery to see if her assistance was needed.

As she passed the half-open door of the big room occupied by the doctor and his wife, she heard voices proceeding from it, and, almost at the same time, some words struck on her ears.

'I don't like Germany's attitude, Madge. Schuschnigg is a fine fellow, but I doubt if he realises the stranglehold Nazi-ism has on the young Austrians. It bothers me a little.'

Robin stuck her fingers in her ears, and raced on down

the long corridor to the big room where the little Russells, together with their young cousins, the Bettanys, and Dr Russell's younger niece, Primula Mary Venables, were curled up round a big armchair pushed to one side. They uttered a shout of joy when they saw Robin, and rushed to meet her. She shut the door, and came among them, laughing at them.

'Robin—Robin! Come and play with us!'

'I came to play with you,' said Robin. 'What have you been doing?'

'Auntie Madge was telling us 'bout Coal-munk-Peter and the Little Glass Man, and Uncle Jem came and called her away,' explained Peggy Bettany, a slim, leggy person of six. '*I* don't know why.'

Robin ruffled the silvery fair curls that covered Peggy's small head. 'Business, I expect. He wouldn't tell you about that, Peg.'

'I don't know,' said Peggy slowly. 'He looked—he looked—oh, I can't 'splain; but it wasn't just bus'ness, I'm sure.'

A severe attack of measles nearly two years before had left Peggy frail for some time, and she had been a good deal with her elders as a consequence. Strong mountain air, rich milk, and regular hours had done a good deal for her; but she still was thin and long, instead of the chubby little bundle she had been. She had also grown much older than her six years warranted, and often made shrewd remarks that startled her elders. On this occasion, Robin looked at her, putting two and two together, and making at least seven of them.

'Supposing Germany starts a war for Austria!' she thought. Then she saw that the small folk were staring at her in amazement, so she hurriedly pulled herself together. 'Let's play Blind Man's Buff,' she suggested. 'Get me a handkerchief from the drawer, Rix, and I'll blindfold you.'

'All right—but not ve babies,' stipulated Rix, Peggy's twin, and as different from her as black curls, velvety brown eyes, and a sturdy little body could make him. 'Vey'll only tumble down an' cry.'

7

'They're quite happy in the corner,' said Robin, glancing at the two. 'Sybil and Jacky, I'm going to pull the table across the corner, and then you'll be quite private by yourselves.'

'Kite pwivate,' echoed Jacky, the youngest member of the Bettany family present—though in India, a little brother and sister known to the Sonnalpe people as 'Second Twins' were beginning to trot all over now, and kept Mother and Ayah in a perpetual state of wondering what mischief they would fall into next.

Robin pulled the table across the corner, shutting in the two youngest members of the nursery party, and then turned to the game, urged thereto by impatient shouts from the rest.

The only child of one of the Russells' greatest friends and a Polish girl who had died of tuberculosis when the child was six, Robin had, for years, been very fragile, and there had been great reason to fear that she might have inherited the dread disease, along with her mother's dark loveliness. But the quiet life at the Sonnalpe, under the constant care of the clever doctors there, whose life-work was the battle against the 'white man's plague,' had overcome her delicacy to a great extent; and though she would never be robust, she was far stronger than anyone had ever hoped.

She was slight and small for her fourteen years, with a mop of black curls framing a softly rosy face of almost angelic beauty. Big brown eyes smiled out from under long lashes, and the firm little chin gave the key to her character. Motherless since early childhood, she had lost her father in January of the previous year through a mountaineering accident. The Russells had been left as her guardians, and she adored them with all the warmth of a warm little heart. As a tiny child, she had addressed them as aunt and uncle. But now that she was fourteen, they had told her to drop the titles, and use the names.

'I won't be addressed as "Guardian" by anyone,' the doctor had declared firmly. 'You're Joey's adopted sister, and Madge is her own sister, and I'm her brother-in-law. It's ridiculous for you to call her "Joey," and us "aunt"

8

and "uncle." So drop it, Rob, and take to our names instead. They're quite good ones,' he had added.

In return for all the loving care lavished on her, the Robin, passionately grateful for the tenderness that would not let her feel alone in the world, did all she could to help in the nursery. In term-time, she attended the Chalet School Annexe, a school established for delicate children high up on the great Sonnenscheinspitze; but a fortnight ago mumps had broken out, and the School had been sent home except for the patients. Robin had, fortunately, escaped the infection, and was now out of quarantine, so she could help once more.

She played with the nursery people till the nursery rang with wild yells and peals of laughter, and Sybil and Jacky crawled out of their corner, under the table, and demanded to be allowed to share in the fun.

'You're too small,' said Master Rix, who ruled the nursery when he got the chance. 'We don't want babies.'

His small cousin Sybil flung herself at him with her chestnut curls flying, and her blue eyes blazing, for Sybil had the temper that goes with red hair, and many were the spars between herself and her masterful cousin.

'*Not* a baby!' she cried, with whirling fists.

Rix knew that he must not hit a girl, however irritating she was, but he grappled with her, and the pair were rolling on the floor, a mass of arms and legs, black and chestnut curls, when the door opened and Mrs Russell herself came in.

'Sybil—Rix!' she exclaimed sternly. 'Are you quarrelling *again*? I shall send you both to bed if this goes on. Get up at once!'

The combatants got to their feet, tousled and panting, and Robin came to the rescue. 'Rix *will* talk about "Babies,"' she said. 'Sybil does hate it, and then she loses her temper and they fight.'

'So I see.' Madge Russell sat down, pulling the pair in front of her. 'Peggy, go and ask Rosa to take them to the bathroom.—Rix, if you call Sybil and Jacky babies again, I'll tie up your mouth for the afternoon.—Sybil, if you fly into another passion, you will go to bed. No crying, children! And no more fighting, or there will be no jam for tea.'

Slightly subdued, the pair went off with Rosa, their nurse, and Mrs Russell sat down in her chair, and looked up at Robin with laughing brown eyes. 'Those two always squabble. I'm afraid Sybs has what Jo describes as "a red-haired temper." Never mind, my Robin. I'm sure *you* couldn't help it.' For Robin was looking rather upset.

'Rix does it to tease,' said his twin. 'But you said we were to go to school next term, Auntie Madge, so he won't tease then.'

Peggy had unbounded belief in school as a reformer. She herself was a gentle, sweet-tempered little soul, most obliging, and quite motherly with the younger ones— though red-headed Sybil sometimes resented the mothering, having a great opinion of herself as the only daughter of the house. She had been known to madden Rix by chanting, '*You're* only a cousin! David an' me *belong*!'

But Robin was not thinking of the children. She sat down on the arm of her guardian's chair, and looked into the sweet face with troubled eyes. 'Madge, I—I overheard something Jem said when I was passing your door just now.'

It was Madge's turn to look disturbed. 'What was it, Robin?'

'About the Nazis,' replied Robin. 'The door was open— I didn't *mean* to hear. I couldn't help it, though.'

'I know that, my pet. Don't worry about it.' Madge glanced across at the little ones who had run off to various ploys of their own. 'Jem feels that he has a good deal of responsibility with the Sanatorium, and the School, too, and he's worried about the way things look like going. That's all. Don't repeat what you heard, Rob,' she added. 'Not even to Joey. We'll be talking about it later, and you only caught a sentence or two. And don't think any more about it.'

'Herr Hitler n'est pas gentil,' observed Robin, dropping into the French that still came most easily to her.

Madge laughed at the expression. 'Scarcely! But there's nothing really to fuss about. Jem's inclined to be a worrier. *I'm* not bothering, and I don't think he need. Now run along and see what Jo's doing. I haven't seen her for hours.'

'She's been writing a new chapter of her book, and then she came to the bathroom to wash her hands,' said Robin, getting up from her perch after dropping a kiss on the curly dark hair just below her. 'I don't know what she's doing now.'

'Then find out, my child!—Little ones, if you come, I'll finish the story I'd begun.'

With shrieks of joy, the little ones left their play and rushed to scramble all over her, reinforced by a clean and tidy Sybil and Rix. Robin laughed, and left the room to hunt for Jo.

Joey proved to be out of the house, so the school-girl only lingered to get into warm coat and beret and gum-boots, before racing out to the garden, where traces of snow still lingered in sheltered nooks and corners, though the lawns were green, and in the beds, scilla and crocus tossed dainty heads in the fresh, February breeze. A bright sun shone bravely down, and the sky was blue, flecked with fluffy white clouds. Calling, 'Joey—Joey!' at the full pitch of a sweet voice, Robin ran down the paths, and finally came on her beloved Jo, standing by the garden wall, looking across the Tiern valley to the great limestone crags that hemmed it in.

'Did you get your hands clean?' demanded Robin as she drew near.

Joey spread out a pair of hands only faintly streaked with ink now. 'Very nearly. What have you been doing, Robinette?'

'Playing with the babies. Sybil and Rix have had a fight,' she added as she reached Joey's side.

'What day don't they? Come along! You aren't supposed to stand about in this wind. It's none too warm yet, for all the sun's shining.' They went up the path, tall Jo, with her delicate, clear-cut face, straight black hair, and glowing black eyes, leading. Not pretty, there was

11

something about her that made people look at her twice. As a child, she had been very fragile. But her years in Tyrol had ended all that and she was now a wiry young person, who rarely ailed anything. All her life she had meant to be a writer, and now she had two books to her credit and was busy with a third.

For the rest, she had been an imp of mischief in her early days at the Chalet School, the institution established by her sister nearly nine years before on the shores of the beautiful Tiern See at the foot of the Sonnenscheinspitze. However, years had brought wisdom, and her last four terms had seen her Head Girl of the School—popular, wise, and showing an understanding probably born of her own naughty Middle days.

She and Robin wandered round the paths, discussing next term with a vim and eagerness that showed that even now Jo Bettany was not so very far removed from the Head Girl. During the summer months, the doctor and his family generally migrated to a big chalet on the shores of the lake, and it was a grievance with the Robin that this year she must spend the term at the Annexe, since now she was strong enough to work the whole term.

'If only I could go back to the Chalet,' she said wistfully. 'I should see something of you then, Jo. But if you're down there, and I am up here, it will not be easy.'

'You'll see plenty of me, my lamb,' declared Joe, with a memory of the last summer, when she had been forced to return to Die Rosen, the Russell home, at least once a week in quest of something urgently needed. 'I never yet contrived to think of all I wanted at a time. I'll be up every week, if not twice or three times."

'It's not the same. When you're up here, I see you every day.'

'Oh, well, you never know what the future may bring forth,' said Jo lightly. 'What time is it? Twelve o'clock? Come along and let's be decent for lunch. I can't very well appear like this, can I?' And she glanced down at

12

her ink-stained skirt, and the soiled blouse-wrists peeping from her coat-sleeves.

'No; and it is not convenable for the doctor's sister to appear so untidy—especially as he may bring guests,' agreed Robin.

'I never was convenable,' said Jo, truthfully enough. 'Oh, well, if you never see me looking any worse, young woman, you'll do well.' Months later, Robin remembered this speech, and first laughed and then shivered. Mercifully, the future was hidden from their eyes for the present, and they went in at the big door of Die Rosen, laughing and making plans for the afternoon.

CHAPTER II

THE CHALET SCHOOL

THE doctor called Jo and Robin downstairs after lunch, just as they were off to get ready for a walk. 'Look here, you two! I'm going down to Briesau to inspect for mumps—not that I think they're likely to get it there; still, prevention is better than cure. If you like to hurry up, you can come with me. But be quick. I won't wait for anyone, and you two are awful slow-coaches sometimes.'

'Insult!' cried Joey indignantly. 'We never keep you waiting—or hardly ever. Of course we'll come. Give us a minute to wash and get into outdoor rig, and we'll be with you at once.'

She vanished as she spoke, to tear along to the bathroom to wash her hands, and came on the Robin doing the selfsame thing.

'I don't know what's wrong with him today,' she said aggrievedly, soaping her hands as she spoke. 'He's like a a bear with a sore paw. Where's the towel?'

Robin tossed it over. 'Here you are. And he hasn't

13

forgotten last week when you kept him waiting thirty-five minutes while you edited that story for the magazine. That's why he's rubbed it in.'

Jo dried her hands perfunctorily and tossed the towel down on the radiator. 'That was only once in a way. And he had only himself to blame for not warning us before that he meant to take us.'

They tore downstairs, wriggling into berets as they went, and tugging on their gloves, and reached the car just in time. The doctor was already in the driving seat. They scrambled in, and he started up.

Along the broad shelf of the Sonnalpe he was obliged to drive slowly, but when they reached the broad coach-road which had been built some years before to link up the place with the Innsbruck-Vienna railway, he let her out, and they went at a terrific pace.

'Are we running a race?' asked Jo, hanging on to the strap. 'Woa, Jem! You'll land us all in a fearful smash if you go on like this.'

'I'm in a hurry,' was all he vouchsafed; and they had to be satisfied with that, and with watching the country-side as it flashed past.

Down the coach road they went, and turned into an-other driving way which went along the side of the rail-road, till it came to the outskirts of Spärtz, the little valley town that lay at the foot of the great crag leading up to the Tiern valley where lies the blue Tiern See, loveliest of all Austria's lovely lakes. Here, at Briesau, a triangular peninsula running from the great Tiern Pass into Germany to the shores of the lake, was the Chalet School.

The School itself consisted of five houses—Ste Thérèse's, the original buildings; St Clare's, St Agnes', St Scholastika's, and St Hild's, the last-named being the Staff Hostel where lived such of the Staff as were not attached to one house or the other.

The main door stood wide, since the day was fine; and just as the car drew up before it, a tall, slender woman appeared, with threads of grey in sunny brown hair, and a clear-cut face lighted by a pair of grey eyes,

14

at present smiling, but, on occasion, stern enough to quell the hardiest offender.

'Dr Jem!' she exclaimed. 'We didn't expect you today as you were down yesterday. No mumps so far, I'm glad to say; and as quarantine time was over yesterday, I don't think we need be afraid now. But I'm very glad to see you,' she added. 'Jo and Robin, too! Come in, all of you. This *will* be an excitement for the School.'

'I thought you were going to Innsbruck today,' said Jo, as she left the car. 'I'm sure you said so when you rang up two days ago.'

'I found I need not go at once, so I'm waiting till Saturday,' explained the Head. 'Robin, don't you want to join the others, mein Blümchen? They are all out on the playing field, though it's rather too muddy for either netball or lacrosse.'

'I should like to go if I may,' replied the Robin. 'Is it French, German, or English day today?"

'French day,' replied the Head. 'Run along, dear. Oh, and if you see Miss Wilson or Miss Stewart, or any of the others, tell them the doctor and Jo are here in my study.'

'Oui, Mademoiselle,' replied the Robin. She made the regulation curtsy demanded of all the girls, and danced off down the corridor

'Come in,' said the Head hospitably, ushering them into her study. 'Nell, or Con, or some of the others will be here shortly, I expect.'

'Look here, Hilda,' said the doctor brusquely, 'I want you to send for the Heads and Seconds of all the Houses. I've come on serious business today.'

The Head, Miss Annersley, to give her her rightful name, raised her brows at this, but all she said was, 'Just ring the bell, please, Jo.'

As for Jo, when she had done as she was asked, she turned on her brother-in-law in some excitement. 'Jem! What's up? What does all this mean? Why——'

Miss Annersley intervened. 'Don't be such a question-mark, Joey! As Con says, you're enough to *deave* anyone when you begin. Sit down, and help yourself to a cigarette.'

Thus suppressed, Jo sat down on the broad window-seat after taking a cigarette, and just then the door opened, and a fair, buxom girl with a pleasant face, attired in the national Tyrolean dress, appeared at the door.

'Oh, Anna, please send Miss Wilson, Miss Stewart, Miss Norman, Miss Soames, Miss Elliot, and Matron Gould to me,' said the Head. Then she looked across at the doctor. 'Do you want Matron Lloyd and Matron Rider, too, Doctor?'

'Yes; and Frau Mieders, and whoever housekeeps at St Hild's, too. Why don't you send for Miss Edwards? I said both of 'em.'

'It's her free day, and she's gone to Spärtz,' explained Miss Annersley. 'Very well, Anna; that is all, thank you.'

Anna curtsied and withdrew, and presently the sound of light footsteps and gay voices told that the Staff were approaching. Jo uncoiled her long legs and rose to her feet as the door opened, and she was characteristically the first to speak.

'Hello, everyone! I've arrived, you see.'

'Joey!' The foremost of them, a very pretty girl, with wavy red-gold hair, delicate colouring, and dark-blue eyes, swept forward. 'My dear girl, don't say that we're sent for just because *you* have taken it into your head to pay us a visit! You aren't Royalty, you know!'

'Don't blame me—blame Jem. It's his doings,' said Jo cheerfully.

A tall, clever-looking woman came across. 'Well, Jo! You haven't come to tell us that you're joining Marie and Wanda and Eugen, have you?'

'Joining Marie and Wanda and Eugen? What in the world do you mean?'

'Haven't you heard? They're all going to America at the end of the week. Eugen's mother was an American, as you ought to know, and Marie and he have had sundry invitations to visit them. They've never gone of course, but after the Gräfin's death, both Marie and Wanda

16

have been run down, so Eugen decided that a nice trip to America would be the very thing for Marie—especially as the baby arrived in the middle of all the trouble. He asked Wanda to go as well, and take Keferl and little Maria Ileana. I believe he wanted Friedel to go too, but Friedel found it impossible to get leave till the summer. So the others are to precede him, and he'll join them for six weeks or so in July. Didn't you really know? I thought Marie would have been sure to tell you. She said she was coming over to say goodbye tomorrow.'

'I haven't had a line. Naturally I thought she hadn't any time, what with little Wolferl, and her mother dying, and everything.'

'They came here to say goodbye yesterday. Marie had the baby with her to let the School see its latest "grandson." The girls were all thrilled. He's a beautiful baby, very like his mother.'

'He would be,' agreed Jo. 'But oh, if Marie is going to be away, I *shall* be lonely this summer! Frieda's gone to Bernhilda at Genoa; Simone is at the Sorbonne still, and won't get away till July at soonest. We four always were a quartette. Now we're being split up, and I don't like it one little bit. Upon my word, Nell, if they ask me, I've a good mind to go with them—if Madge will let me.'

'What's that?' demanded the doctor from across the room.

'Marie and Co. are all going to America on Saturday,' said Jo with a groan.

'They are going to America? When?'

'At the end of the week. If they ask me, may I go?'

'You'll get no invitation on such short notice—unfortunately.'

'Well! Of all the nice, kind, brotherly remarks! Are you so anxious to be rid of me?'

'I'd give a good deal to know that you and Madge, and all the children, including the Robin, were all well out of the country,' replied the doctor.

A gasp went round the room. He took no notice, but merely went on: 'I've sent for you folk to tell you that

17

the School has to be moved up to the Sonnalpe at once. Your half-term comes next week-end, doesn't it, Hilda? then you can just get ready, and everything will go while the girls are away. How long are you giving them?'

'Five days. This is a long term,' replied Miss Annersley mechanically. 'We break up on Thursday morning, and don't return till Tuesday evening.'

'But—but *why*?' demanded the red-haired girl, who was Miss Stewart, the history mistress. 'What's going to happen? Why this sudden removal?'

'I don't like the trend affairs are taking,' he told them quietly. 'I'm afraid of Germany's demands on Austria. I think she's going to try to bring Austria into the Reich. It's very likely. It *may* mean war, though I scarcely think so. I doubt if Miklas and Schuschnigg would involve their country in what could only prove to mean appalling bloodshed, and, unless someone backs Austria, ultimate failure. But do you realise that if Germany does do this, it would mean the establishment of their confounded Gestapo, and probable unpleasantness for such a place as the Chalet School?'

There was silence as the women seated round the room digested this.

'Surely they wouldn't dare to interfere with us?' said Miss Annersley uncertainly. 'We aren't nationals. Germany doesn't want trouble with Britain—not yet, at any rate. Oh, I know they hate us. They hate all democracies, of course.'

'I don't say they would interfere openly,' said the doctor. 'But if you broke any of their wretched rules and regulations, it might mean trouble. If that happened —well, you are all women, with no menfolk to defend you as long as you remain here. If you were at the Sonnalpe, there are seven of us British doctors, not to mention the men of the English colony. I should feel happier about you.'

'What do Madame and Mademoiselle say?' demanded Miss Wilson.

'They agree with me, though I must admit Madge thinks I'm making a fuss about nothing. Still, she thinks

that as I *am* worried, the School had better be moved—
and at once. If we give you all the help we can, can
you possibly move during the half-term?'

'Yes; if we all stay—or most of us,' said Miss Annersley. 'Ivy can't, as she's taking the British girls to Innsbruck; and one or two other people are on week-end duty
in other places. But otherwise, we can manage it.'

'But,' began Miss Norman shyly, 'how do you know
that Germany has anything up her sleeve? There was
nothing in the papers this morning and nothing came
over the radio—at least, nothing more than usual.'

'That may be so. But Hitler is speaking of including
all the German-speaking peoples on the continent in the
Reich—says it's only the full return of the full cycle of
history. What he doesn't seem to have grasped,' went
on the doctor, 'is that the Holy Roman Empire, as such,
was a very loosely woven affair, in which the various
states and principalities were always at feud with one
another. To drag all the modern states under one form
of government, which seems to be his purpose, *isn't*
reviving the old Empire. However, you'll never get a
monomaniac to see anything he doesn't want to see.
And I distrust his methods. So, just prepare——'

'Are we to let the girls know?' asked Miss Stewart.

'No; the fewer who know the better. I don't want
any talk if it can be avoided, until the thing is done.'

'That's wise,' said Matron gravely. 'But how are we
to manage?'

'Easily. How many days of the week pass without at
least one or two of you coming up to the Sonnalpe?
I'll send the car each day, as the thaw is making the
roads impossible. You must contrive to pack in what you
can and bring it up with you. André shall bring it, as
I don't think we'll risk any driving but his on such
treacherous roads. Oh, I'm not being insulting. It was all
I could do to keep out of skids'—Joey opened her
mouth to protest at this, but thought better of it and
shut it again—'and I have stronger wrists than any of
you people. No one will be surprised. There's general
grousing round the district at the state of road-surface.'

19

'There's one thing I should like to know,' observed Miss Wilson at this point. 'And that is, where are we going? The Annexe won't take even a quarter of us. We have two hundred and eleven girls this term. I may be in error, but I always thought the Annexe was built to hold fifty at most, and there are—how many up there now?'

'Twenty-seven,' said Joey, speaking for the first time. 'And Juliet and Grizel, of course.'

'Exactly. Well, where are *we* to be parked, then?'

'Do you remember Der Edel Ritter, that new hotel that was opened last August by a Herr Eiser from Bonn?''

There was a chorus of assent.

'Herr Eiser died three weeks ago,'' said the doctor gravely. 'His widow wishes to return to her own people at Bonn. She was telling me about it, and I told her that I might wish to make an addition to the Sanatorium, so would buy the place from her if she cared to let me have it. We struck the bargain last week. Naturally, until I see how things are likely to go, I'm taking no more patients, so Der Edel Ritter will not be needed for that purpose for the next few months. I'm going to park the School there.'

'Well, it's large enough,' agreed Matron. 'There must be a hundred and fifty bedrooms; and all the other places on the ground-floor. If you'd tried for fifty years, I doubt if you could have got a more suitable place.'

'But what about games?'' demanded Miss Stewart.

'There are six tennis-courts. Also, I've bought that bit of rough grassland at the back of the hotel, and I'm having it turfed over for cricket. There's a swimming-pool—Herr Eiser was nothing if not modern, and he knew such things would attract a good many people—and a gymnasium, fully fitted up. The games side of the affair isn't going to be much trouble.'

'But,' said Joey, saying aloud the question most people were burning to ask, but had too much tact to voice, '*how* do you know there's likely to be trouble just now, Jem? As Ivy says, there's been nothing come out in the papers or the radio. Why this sudden agitation?'

The doctor looked round at them thoughtfully, considering them. They were all honourable women. He decided to entrust them with a part of a secret he had intended to keep in its entirety.

'I have a friend in Wiesbaden,' he began abruptly. 'Some weeks ago he came to consult with me about a case of his that is here. We met at the Europe, and as a blizzard began that afternoon, we had to stay down there. The place happened to be full, so we were obliged to share a bedroom. He knows, of course, that we have a tremendous responsibility with regard to the School, with its mixed-grill of nationalities. As we were together, and it would have been almost impossible for anyone to overhear us, he warned me then that in high official circles in Germany, there was more than a talk of an Anschluss. He dared not say much: the Gestapo has its agents everywhere. But he told me that if he saw any reason to suppose that Hitler meant to strike, he would write to me, and in the letter would be two words that doctors use occasionally, which would mean nothing to anyone who didn't know, but would mean to me that danger was at hand. That letter came this morning—and it had been delayed two or three days.' He ceased, and there was a silence that could be felt.

'What about the visiting Staff?' asked Matron Lloyd, a tall young Welshwoman, who was responsible for the domestic side of St Agnes'.

'I shall let Anserl and Laubach know. Denny and Miss Denny will find a home with us'—Jo groaned loudly at this, but no one took any notice, so she subsided—'How many more are there?'

'Herr von Borken comes for 'cello, and Herr Helfen for harp,' said Miss Annersley promptly. 'Everyone else is either in the School or at St Hild's, I think. Isn't that so, Frau Mieders?' She turned to a fair, pleasant-looking Austrian, hitherto silent, who was head of the Staff Hostel, St. Hild's.

'Quite correct,' replied Frau Mieders. 'But if it is as

21

the Herr Doktor thinks, then I must consider my mother and my little sister in Kufstein. Almost certainly, the towns will be the first to suffer. Herr Doktor, what am I to do?' She looked at him, anxiety in her eyes.

'We will invite Frau Kalkmann and the little Lieserl to spend a few weeks with us,' he replied promptly. 'Let us get our plans for the School made, and then, meine Frau, we will see what can be arranged. One of us will drive you over to Kufstein in the Hispano-Suiza, and bring them back. Frau Kalkmann can bring any valuables with her, and she must shut up her house. I intend to offer Herr Laubach and his wife the little chalet where my office is,' he added. 'We must send down an ambulance for her. I only wish,' he added, 'that we could bring all our friends safely to the Sonnalpe. But it is impossible.'

'Tante Gisel is staying with Gisela and Gottfried,' Jo reminded him. 'Onkel Florian won't want to leave his business though,' she added sorrowfully. 'What about Onkel Reise and Tante Gretchen?'

'They are going to Bernhilda and Kurt, so they will be safe for the present. Well, I think that's all we can do. Miss Annersley, I must discuss a few details with you. Shall we meet the rest at Kaffee und Kuchen at the usual hour? Then Jo can go off and join the girls. —And mind you hold your tongue, Jo,' he added sternly. 'Remember, I am trusting you to say nothing. If we can make this removal a *fait accompli* before any outsiders get wind of it, so much the better.'

'You won't do that,' said Jo, preparing to follow the Staff out of the room. 'You can't move furniture on the quiet, and the furniture you'll have to move.'

'Only the actual school furnishings,' he said. 'I took over the furniture at Der Edel Ritter with the place. As for the rest—we'll see.'

Jo turned to leave the room, whither the Staff had preceded her.

'You know, this is the most thrilling event I've ever known. I'd no idea we were going to be mixed up in such a penny-dreadful, shilling-shocker thing as the secret police of *any* country! I ought to get a book out of this!' She fled, laughing.

'Jo can't take this thing seriously,' said the doctor almost sadly, as the door closed behind her. 'It's just as well, perhaps. I foresee a tough row for us to hoe. Well, now to business, Hilda!'

CHAPTER III

THE SCHOOL LEARNS THE NEWS

'I HAVE feelin's,' remarked Hilary Burn, Head Girl of the Chalet School, mysteriously.

'What, then?' asked her great friend, Jeanne le Cadoulec, the Games Captain, turning serious eyes of Breton blue on her.

These two, together with sundry other grandees of the prefects, were sharing a compartment. Normally, they would have been required to take charge of various compartments of Middles and Juniors; but on this occasion the Staff had turned up in full force, and the Upper Sixth had been bidden keep together, and never mind their Juniors.

'So much the better for us!' remarked Evadne Lannis, an American of almost seventeen, to her own special chum, Cornelia Flower. And Cornelia, speaking from the vantage-point of sixteen and a half, and a very new prefectship, had answered gravely, 'I guess you're right.' So here they all were, very select indeed, and somewhat crowded, since, as prefects, they felt it their right to be together, and send the rest of the Upper and Lower Sixths next door.

Now, when Hilary spoke, they all looked at her with one accord. 'What's up?' demanded Evadne. 'How do you mean—feelings?'

'Well, have you noticed that *all* the Staff are on escort duty, with the exception of the Head, the Matrons, and Nally?''

23

'I knew it, of course,' replied Jeanne. 'What then, my Hilary? It is not, after all, so surprising.'

'Surprising enough. When did they ever do such a thing before? Usually, they send down two junior mistresses, and expect us to help in keeping order. Why this strong bodyguard today, I wonder?'

Maria Marani, a short, bright-faced Innsbrucker of seventeen, with a long black pigtail and sparkling dark eyes, looked serious. 'I wonder,' she began uncertainly, 'I wonder—if——'

'If—what?' demanded Cornelia, for Maria had stopped short.

'It is just—Dr Jem came down to see Papa, and they talked very gravely. Papa sent word to Mamma that she is to stay with Gisela at the Sonnalpe for the present. And he said if it had not been so near the end of the holiday, he would have sent me to Gisela, also.'

'But why?' demanded Jeanne. 'Is there, then, some infectious illness breaking out in Innsbruck?'

'Yes,' said Giovanna, a fair-haired, German-looking girl of their own age. 'There is. But *you* needn't worry, Jeanne. It's never likely to trouble you—or Hilary, or Corney and Evvy, either,' she added rather cryptically.

'Queer disease if it attacks some people and leaves others alone,' added Hilary sceptically. 'Whose leg are you trying to pull?'

'Nobody's,' said Giovanna stormily. 'And as for the disease, it comes from *Germany*, and won't attack anyone who knows what *freedom* means! My father says so!'

'If,' began Hilary, 'you mean——' She got no further. At that moment, a little thin woman, with the face of a weasel, who had been passing in time to hear Giovanna's remark, deliberately turned back, and stared through the glassed-in door of the compartment, evidently trying to see who had spoken.

'Gardez-vous!' hissed Jeanne, while a tall girl, whose chief characteristics were a magnificent tail of chestnut hair dangling down her back, honest grey eyes, and a long, obstinate chin, calmly rose from her place, and stood against the door, blocking the view completely.

Baffled, the spy moved on, with a lingering glance through one of the windows; but it had given the girls a shock. Giovanna was pale, and Hilary's dark grey eyes blazed.

'I forgot that there seem to be spies everywhere,' she said in an undertone. 'We ought to have kept watch, of course. Gio, don't look like that. If she comes back, she'll know it's you by your looks. As it is, thanks to Polly's quickness, I don't believe she could make out. All the same, Polly,' she added severely, 'you were abominably rude.'

'And what was she?' demanded Polly, as she squeezed into her seat again. 'How dared she stare at us like that? She hasn't *bought* the train, has she?'

'I'm afraid it was what Giovanna was saying,' said Hilary reluctantly. 'Gio, you *must* be careful how you talk in public. I've read that the Gestapo have spies everywhere in Austria and Czecho-Slovakia as well as Germany. Dad says old Hitty wants the whole earth, and we are very near. Be careful, all of you.'

'Let us all sit forward, so that we can hide Giovanna,' suggested Jeanne brilliantly. 'If she comes back, she cannot see her then.'

'Good idea! And Gio, change places with Evva, just in case.'

Sure enough, the spy did return. But all she got for her pains was the sight of a cluster of heads, all nodding together; and if she listened, it is fairly safe to assume that what she heard was Greek to her, for the girls were discussing lacrosse with vigour.

This lasted till they reached Spärtz, where they swung themselves down from the carriages, and formed up on the platform in three long files, expectant of being marched out of the station, and up the woodland path to the Tiernthal.

Greatly to their astonishment, they found, when they got outside the station, that big buses awaited them, and they were seated therein, and driven away at speed.

'What on earth is happening?' cried Hilary. 'Miss Wilson,' to that lady, who had found a seat in their bus, 'why are we busing instead of walking? What's the idea? Is the path blocked, or anything?'

Miss Wilson shook her head. 'Not so far as I know. I have some news for you, girls. We have moved the Chalet School up to the Sonnalpe.' She paused a moment, and then hurried on. 'I know you will be pleased, for it means that we shall see more of Mademoiselle Lepattre. Besides that, Madame proposes to renew her English literature classes to the top forms.'

'Good-o!' cried Evadne. 'I've always heard her classes were bully, though I wasn't old enough to join them when she left. But now we'll all be in them. I call that something like news!'

'And we'll see Mademoiselle,' added Cornelia. 'That's the best news I've heard in a twelvemonth.'

Cornelia was a motherless girl, and until the serious illness of Mlle Lepattre, now almost two years before, had had most of her 'mothering' from the former Head of the School. She had been a firebrand in her early days, and Mademoiselle's invariable kindness had gone deep. When the news came that the Head Mistress would teach no more, Corney, as they all called her, had suffered bitterly, though she had said little.

Miss Wilson nodded. 'Yes; I thought it would please you. There's another thing,' she added. 'We have taken in the Annexe, of course, and those of you who have sisters up there will now be in school with them.'

'And so many of our old girls live up there, too,' murmured Jeanne rather sentimentally. 'Gisela, and Bette, and Gertrud——'

'And Juliet and Grizel at the Annexe,' added Evadne. 'Say, Miss Wilson, will they teach *us*?'

'Miss Carrick certainly will, Miss Cochrane will have only a few of you for music,' returned Miss Wilson primly. 'But, of course, Miss Carrick will be leaving at the end of this term to be married. It has been arranged that the wedding shall take place the last day of term so that as many of you as possible may be present.'

'Where will it be?' asked Polly. 'In Innsbruck?'

'No; in the little Anglican church at the Sonnalpe.'

26

'Oh, Miss Wilson,' exclaimed Hilary at this point, 'we had such a funny experience in the train.'

'How do you mean, Hilary?' asked Miss Wilson quickly. 'What was it?'

Briefly, Hilary told the story, and Miss Wilson listened with a frown. When it was ended, she said, 'Well, let that be a warning to all of you not to repeat conversations you've overheard, and not to abuse other people so loudly that utter strangers turn to see who you are.'

'But, Miss Wilson,' protested Hilary; then, encountering what she afterwards described as 'a Medusa-like glare,' she fell silent.

The prefects were not distracted from their own views; but the rest of the two Sixths who were sharing the bus with them, thought no more of the incident. They were far too much excited about the new prospect to heed the fact that some stranger had looked in at the prefects as they talked on the train.

'Miss Wilson, will Robin Humphries be with us?' asked a French girl in her own language, since it was still holiday time.

'Naturally,' replied Miss Wilson absently. 'She's a pupil at the Annexe, as you know, Yvette. She, and Lorenz Maïco, and Amy Stevens will all be with us again.'

'I am glad,' said Yvette; 'especially about Amy. I was so sorry when she got that cold last winter, and had to go back to the Annexe.'

'So was Amy. She's looking forward to seeing you all.'

'Will Jo come and teach us again?' asked someone else.

'I doubt it, Hilda. She only helped us for the term, you know, and she never really liked teaching.'

'But where exactly are we going?' demanded Polly. 'There isn't a place big enough up there for us all, is there?'

'Do you remember that new hotel, Der Edel Ritter? That is the School now.'

'Der Edel Ritter? That *huge* place?' cried Evadne. 'Why, they've covered courts for tennis and badminton,

27

and a gorgeous swimming-pool and a gym, and everything! How simply—amazing!'

'But what about science?' demanded Luise Rotheim, an Austrian girl who was one of Miss Wilson's 'star' pupils in this subject. 'Where are we going to have science? And what about geography? Have you made a new room for it, Miss Wilson?'

'We have fitted up one of the garages for chemistry,' explained Miss Wilson. 'As for geography, I'm afraid you'll have to be content with lessons in your form-rooms, just as we did three years ago, Luise. We hope to have a geography room prepared for next term.'

So they chattered on, until the buses took the slope of the great coach-road, which told them that they were nearing their destination. Then they fell silent for the most part, until they were running through the broad shelf of the Sonnalpe. Then they began to talk again, this time of a very important point.

'If we are all in one house, Miss Wilson, how can we be divided up into houses?' asked Jeanne.

'Easily, as it happens. Der Edel Ritter was built with a centre portion, and two wings. And there is the Annexe. We shall keep our four houses, the central part being Ste Thérèse's, the right wing St Clare's, and the left St Scholastika's. The Annexe becomes St Agnes', which has always been the smallest of the houses, as you all know. So when we arrive, we shall meet in hall—the main lounge, it was—and then you will march to your various houses, just as usual. Upstairs, you will find lists on the doors, so that you can easily know your dormitories. Prefects and House Prefects have rooms to themselves. Each house has its own common-room; and there is a very pleasant Prefects' room. I left Jo and Robin busy with the library, which is in Ste Thérèse's. A big room in St Clare's has been given over to the school orchestra; and St Scholastika's has a special room for the Hobbies Club.'

'And what has St. Agnes'?' demanded Suzanne Mercier, who was Head Prefect of St Agnes', and very jealous for the honour of her house.

28

'That has been given the fiction library, Suzanne. You will have to make arrangements with your own prefects about library duty. Now, the new school is in sight; and there are Jo and Robin waiting for us at the gate.'

Two minutes later, the Senior bus had drawn up before the hotel, and the girls were scrambling out, ready to take charge as the Middles and the Juniors tumbled down from their buses. Joey had come racing to join them; and as the first Middles bus discharged its load, Robin seized on two or three old friends, and was talking hard as she led them into the new school.

Such a noise the Sonnalpe had never heard before, and quite a crowd of inhabitants were gathered at the gates to see the girls arrive. The girls were welcomed by Miss Annersley, who met them smiling as if no cold dread lay at her heart, for Dr Jem had succeeded in infecting her with his own fears by this time. But, joyous as their greetings to her were, they were eclipsed when the door to the lounge opened and Mrs Russell, slim, girlish-looking despite her family, and beautiful, entered among them, on her arm, a sallow, plain-faced lady, whose face was marked with deep lines drawn there by pain. Then, indeed, the School let itself go, as the girls gave rousing cheers for 'Madame' and 'Mademoiselle'! Miss Annersley laughed, and let them have their vent for a few minutes. Then she clapped her hands for silence, and when she had obtained it, she invited Mrs Russell to speak to the girls.

Her face a little touched with deeper colour than its wont, her eyes glowing, Madge Russell came forward. 'I bid you all welcome to the new school, girls,' she said, her low-pitched, clear voice reaching to the farthest corner of the great room. 'I hope we shall have many very happy times here, and that this new Chalet School will prove to be as happy, as healthy, and as successful as the Chalet School we have left. In the valley, we used to tell you to let your thoughts rise to the hills. Now we are on the hills themselves, I tell you to keep your thoughts high. To rise, so that you may help to set right wrongs; to show the way, so far as in any of us lies, to the kind of world God meant this to be when He gave it to man. Be upright; be honest; be brave. Courage is a great thing, and we do not know how soon we may need it, nor how far we may have to strain it in the days ahead. So take this for your motto for the rest of this year: "Be brave!"'

She finished, and after another cheer, and the singing of the school hymn, the girls were dismissed to seek their dormitories and tour the building.

Said fourteen-year-old Betty Wynne-Davies to her special chum, Elizabeth Arnett, 'What on earth was Madame getting at? I didn't understand it one little bit. Why *should* we need to be brave?'

'Oh, it's just the usual Head's talk. They've got to say something moral. It was better than most things, anyhow,' said Elizabeth. 'Come on! I want to find our dormy and settle in!'

Hilary, left alone with Jeanne and Giovanna, looked at them. 'That *meant* something! "Be brave!" I wonder just how brave we shall all have to be? But, at least, let's play the game by the School. Before everything else, let's remember that we're Chalet girls, and that Chalet girls hang together even though they're far enough apart at times.'

CHAPTER IV

THE CHALET SCHOOL PEACE LEAGUE

THE girls soon settled down to work and play in their new quarters. Luckily, the syllabus for parallel forms in the two branches of the School had been alike, so that there was little difficulty there. Miss Carrick had seen to it that her own girls kept more or less level with their own forms in the Chalet School, so it was an easy matter to fit them in. But mark-books and form registers meant some hours of work.

Mrs Russell, with no baby on her hands now, took up her old lectures on English literature, and so relieved pressure a little. Then Joey was pressed into service. She grumbled at having to give up two mornings a week; but she dared not refuse. The Annexe Staff took over some lessons, though Miss Carrick was largely freed that she might hasten the preparations for her wedding at the end of term.

She had been engaged nearly four years—Joey always took the credit for that engagement—and her fiancé, a barrister attached to the Dublin High Court, was now making a very fair income, and Juliet had never been accustomed to an extravagant way of living.

Meantime, affairs outside the School were moving quickly. The Middles, absorbed in their own life, paid little heed to it; but the elder girls, many of whom were Austrians, watched what was happening with hearts in many cases beginning to feel a little dread.

'What will happen?' demanded Maria Marani fearfully one day early in March. 'Papa does not allow Mamma to return home. He has sent up here many of our treasures. Yet he will not come himself. Oh, what is going to happen?'

Three days later came Dr Schuschnigg's announcement of the plebiscite demanded by Germany. Herr Marani came up to the Sonnalpe that day, and he was full of despair as he talked to the doctors and Mrs Russell after Mittagessen.

'What can we do? My poor country! What will happen to thee?'

'It may settle down all right,' said one of the younger doctors, Jack Maynard, consolingly. 'Don't you think so, Gottfried?'

Gottfried Mensch, brother of Jo's great friend, Frieda Mensch, and husband of Herr Marani's elder girl, Gisela, once the Head Girl of the School, shook his head. 'God above knows! I am thankful the father and mother and little Frieda are safely out of the country. I wish I could send Gisela and the children to join them.'

31

Dr Maynard looked thoughtful. 'What about the School?' he asked.

'I am afraid,' said Mrs Russell quietly, 'that this will mean a big loss to the School. Parents of other nationalities will not be anxious to send us their children if Germany—or rather, Nazi-ism—is in the saddle.'

'I doubt if they will interfere with any but Austrian and German girls, Madame,' said another young Austrian doctor. 'Germany does not wish any trouble with the other nations—yet.'

'But it will come,' said Madge, nodding her head wisely. 'Oh, I wish one could see into the future!'

On the eleventh of March came Dr Schuschnigg's final speech, and Germany marched in and took possession. Austria, as Austria, was no more. She was merely a province of the Greater Reich.

Mercifully, up on the Sonnalpe, they were free for some weeks from more than the merest official visitation. One day, Dr Russell was summoned to meet representatives of the German local government. He found the men very decent fellows on the whole, full of admiration for the great work done at the Sanatorium. Indeed, one of them went out of his way to do the Sonnalpe a good turn. Taking an opportunity when his two companions were examining the great 'iron lung' which had just been established, he called the head of the place to one side.

'Herr Doktor,' he said in rapid undertones, 'be advised by me. Get rid of your Austrians, and then the Government will not interfere with you. But so long as they are with you, you may meet with molestation. And bid your gnädige Frau to dismiss her Austrian teachers and all Austrian and German girls. Now, no more.' Then he added aloud, 'It is a great work, Herr Doktor, and greatly performed.'

That night, Jem Russell called a conference of the Staffs of both School and Sanatorium, and laid before them the remarks of the friendly Nazi.

'Needless to say,' he concluded, 'neither my wife nor I wish you to go. But there is the question of whether employment with us may not mean trouble for any of Austrian or German birth. So I think you ought to know and consider what you will do.'

Herr Anserl growled, shaking his great shaggy head. 'I am an old man, mein Sohn. I stay where I am. I say that it is an iniquitous thing if a man cannot choose his own employers.'

Gottfried Mensch, very white, and with bright eyes, agreed. 'But,' he added, 'I am sending Gisela and the children out of the country at once. Few know these mountains as I do. I am getting them by means of a way known to few into Switzerland, thence to France, and so to England.'

Frau Mieders sighed. 'I must stay where I am. My mother and Lieserl will also remain.'

'As we will,' said Herr Laubach, the art master.

Von Ahlen, the young Austrian, then spoke. 'My father was murdered in one of the riots in Wien five years ago. I am no Nazi. I will stay.'

But where the girls were concerned, it was a different matter. Before long, parents, obviously acting under stress of orders from the Government, wrote for their girls to return home. Herr Marani defied the order: Maria should stay where she was. There was no other school at the Sonnalpe for her to attend, and her home would be there for the future, he declared.

This was during the Easter holidays, after which a much smaller School would return, as Madge had predicted.

But before they had broken up, the girls themselves had held a meeting, headed by Hilary, Jeanne, Evadne, Giovanna, Ilonka, and Robin. They had solemnly formed a peace league among themselves, and vowed themselves to a union of nations, whether they should ever meet again or not.

'Let us all remember that we are the Chalet School,' said Hilary, her lips quivering, as she looked at Giovanna, who was leaving them.

Giovanna winked back the tears from her eyes. 'I, for one, will never forget it,' she said. 'I am no Nazi,

33

and I hate them because of what they are doing. Our dear School!' And she burst into tears.

She was not the only one. Of the two hundred odd who met that night, only one hundred and thirty would be returning. The rest were either to go to Nazi schools, or remain in their own countries for education. Only Maria sat with head uplifted, cheeks flushed, eyes flashing.

'I stay,' she said firmly. 'Papa and Mamma are agreed.'

So the Chalet School League was formed, and signed by every girl there. Then came the question of what to do with the paper. The girls had heard too much of what might happen to dare to risk leaving it open. Many of the girls were well on in their teens, and, from all accounts, Hitler and his crew were perfectly capable of punishing them. Already there were whispers of concentration camps. The great Jewish millionaire, Count Louis Rothschild, was imprisoned. Dr Schuschnigg was under arrest, and so were many others of the party.

Robin solved the problem. 'We'll put it in our cave,' she said. 'Some of us can go there tomorrow, and there is a place I know where it will take no harm.'

'We must make a picnic,' said Jeanne, forgetting her English in her excitement. 'Tomorrow is Saturday. Let us make a picnic——'

'And ask Joey to come, too!' added Evadne. 'She ought to sign our League, I guess, if anyone does. Joey is the—the—the *spirit* of the School. You know what I mean!'

The girls were all agreed, though Evvy's meaning was not very clearly expressed. Joey certainly should sign with the rest of them. They sent Robin to seek her, and presently she came, very grave, and unusually grown-up for her.

'We are forming a League, Joey,' said Hilary, going straight to the point. 'We want you to join with us, and sign, too. Will you?'

'Let me see what you've written,' said Jo, holding out her hand.

Hilary gave it to her, and she read it slowly.

'We, the girls of the Chalet School, hereby vow ourselves members of the Chalet School League. We swear faithfully to do all we can to promote peace between all our countries. We will not believe any lies spoken about evil doings, but we will try to get others to work for peace as we do. We will not betray this League to any enemy, whatever may happen to us. If it is possible, we will meet at least once a year. And we will always remember that though we belong to different lands, we are members of the Chalet School League of Peace.'

Then there followed a long list of names.

'It's a good plan,' said Jo, wrinkling up her brows, 'but I doubt how far we'll be able to keep it. So many of the girls are so young.'

'But we are all members of the School!' cried Maria.

'Yes; but I don't know how long the Juniors will feel that. You may be sure that once they are sent to Nazi schools they'll be taught to hate the place. Oh, I'll sign it!' And Jo produced her fountain-pen, and dashed off her signature at the foot of the list. 'What about the Staff—and the other old girls? Oughtn't you to get them to join too?'

'You cannot ask the people in Germany,' said Giovanna, choking down her sobs. 'It would not be fair to them, and it would tell the Nazis what we are doing. But the others—yes.'

So it was decided. Jo was to write cautiously to such of the old girls as were out of the Reich, and the Staff were to be asked to join, too. It was bedtime for the Juniors before things were finally settled. Then Jo invited certain of them to come for a picnic with her on the morrow, that they might go to what was known as 'Robin's Cave,' since Robin had discovered it, and hide the document there.

'Sorry I can't ask the lot of you,' said Jo cheerfully, 'but the cave wouldn't long remain a secret if everyone knew. By the way, Dr Jack must come with us. We aren't allowed to go by ourselves.'

The precious document was entrusted to her, and the School went to Prayers feeling—the older portion of it—much more cheerful than it had done. They did not know what might lie before them in the future, but at least they would remain united, and that would be some comfort.

CHAPTER V

SPIED ON!

THE next day, after Mittagessen, a merry party set out, headed by Jo and the young doctor, who had agreed to come with them with delight. He had known Jo since her stormy youth; had seen her grow up and, for the last two years, had been quite decided about what she meant to him. Whether Jo would look on things in the same light or not was another matter. She had grown up in a land where the girls marry early. Already, many of those who had been at school with her were wives and mothers. Her own beloved friend, Marie von Eschenau, had been wedded at the age of eighteen. Simone Lecoutier, another of their quartette, was at the Sorbonne, but had confided in Jo about a certain young officer of the artillery, who was urgent that she should settle down with him to army life. As for Frieda Mensch, the last of the four, Jo guessed that young Dr von Ahlen asked nothing better than to carry off the pretty sister of his friend and colleague, Gottfried Mensch. And Jo had her own suspicions of Frieda's attitude. But so far, despite this, Jo remained the complete schoolgirl for most purposes.

With them came Robin Humphries, Hilary Burn, Jeanne le Cadoulec, and the two American girls, Evadne Lannis and Cornelia Flower. Ilonka Barkocz, who was to have made one of the party, had wakened that morning with a violent attack of toothache, which had been followed by an early visit to the Sonnalpe dentist, Herr von Francius. Giovanna, also invited, had refused sadly.

'I had better not know. But I do hope it will be safe where you hide it, and I will pray that you may not be spied on while you are doing it.'

'Poor Giovanna,' said Joey, as she and Jack Maynard strolled up the mountain path, talking idly. 'I'm sorry for her. She's in a horrid position. But I do see her point, and I think she's right.'

'So do I,' said the doctor soberly. 'The less she really knows the better.'

Jo turned to him. 'Jack! Do you think Austria's in for a bad time?'

'With Himmler's Gestapo everywhere? Use your common sense, Jo! And beware what you say,' he added. 'Your voice carries.'

'Right you are,' agreed Jo amiably. 'I wonder if we've *really* got everything this time? We never yet set out on a picnic that we didn't leave *something* behind! Did you put in the salt for the eggs?'

'I did—and also the flasks of coffee which I found standing in the hall. You owe me one for that, Jo.'

'Oh, there's a spring up there. We shouldn't have died of thirst,' said Jo airily. 'Thanks, all the same. We turn off here,' she added, pulling him into a side-track which looked more like a goat-track than a reasonable path for human beings.

'I've never been this way,' he said as he obeyed her. 'Do the rest know we turn here, or should we wait for them and warn them? It might be as well to send them on in front. Then we can keep an eye on their doings. Evvy and Corney have always been stormy petrels.'

'Once,' said Jo. 'They're sane beings now.'

'Still, I think we'll have them in front if you don't mind. Cooey!'

His cry was answered by a distant 'Cooey!' and then the other five came racing up, their hands full of early spring flowers.

'You five trot on in front,' said the doctor. 'Then Jo and I can keep an eye on you and be prepared to risk our necks if you risk yours.'

'As if we should!' began Hilary heatedly. Then she stopped, and stared.

From among the trees, already showing veils of delicate green, came a small, wiry-looking woman, together with a little boy of about nine.

'Frau Eisen and little Hermann!' exclaimed Jo under her breath. 'Oh, well, we haven't bought up the mountain. But I thought they'd left three days ago.' She bowed to the woman, giving her the pretty Tyrolean greeting, 'Grüss Gott!'

'Heil Hitler!' piped up the urchin, much to their amazement; for this was the first time they had heard the Nazi greeting out of Germany.

His mother looked annoyed. 'Hush, Hermann!' she said. 'Silence, naughty one! Nay; silence, I say!' as he opened his lips to speak.

He was silent, but a sullen look overspread his face, and his grey eyes glowered at the girls as they passed. Jo glanced at him, a queer expression on her face, though she said nothing. Then they were out of earshot, and the five girls came round them.

'Did you hear *that*?' cried Evadne. 'That kid gave the Nazi greeting!'

Hilary's brows were knitted, and her lips were set in a straight line. 'That is the woman that spied on us in the train,' she said.

'Frau Eisen?' Jo gave vent to a long, low whistle.

'What are you driving at, Joey,' demanded Cornelia Flower, her big blue eyes widening.

'Only that Jem swears that woman's a Nazi dyed in the wool. I *wonder*!—Rob, what do you think? You know her, don't you?'

Robin nodded. 'She is rude—but *very* rude,' she said. 'When Madge called on her, she was most rude, though Herr Eisen was very polite.'

Jo turned to the others. 'How much did that woman hear of what Gio was saying in the train?'

Hilary shook her head. 'I couldn't tell you.—Jeanne, do *you* know?'

A troubled look came into Jeanne's eyes. 'A good deal, I fear. But I do not think she knew who said it. And when she came again, we were all with our heads close, talking of lacrosse. And Giovanna had changed her seat, also.—Does it matter, Joey?'

Instead of replying, Jo turned to the doctor. 'What about it, Jack?'

'Couldn't tell you. It all depends on what she is. If, as I'm inclined to think, she's a spy for the Gestapo, it may mean trouble for Giovanna. How old is the kid, by the way?'

'She's seventeen and a bit—I don't know how much. About my age,' replied Hilary. 'Why?'

'Because Joey fears she may be in danger of—well, what they call preventive arrest. If that woman didn't see her, it may be all right. But if we've got someone like that in the village, I'd advise all you girls to be careful what you are saying.'

They were speaking in English, and in undertones. There was a little silence after the doctor's last words, which was broken by a sudden 'cr-r-rack!' which made Robin raise her head sharply, and stare in the direction of a clump of bushes to the right hand. Startled, the others followed her gaze. Evadne's quick eyes picked out a piece of grey jacket peeping round one side. She would have sprung forward but the doctor saw it at the same time, and caught her arm.

'No, Evvy. The kid's got as much right there as we have. You'll only have a row for no purpose. Instead, let's go on. And do look, girls, as though this *were* a pleasure trip,' he added. 'Let them think that we're only discussing the contents of the baskets, or anything rather than what we *have* been discussing.' Then, raising his voice, he added, 'Told you so! Now, perhaps, you'll agree that I'm a better packer for picnics than you are, Joey my child!'

Joey was quick to take his cue. 'Oh, well, apologies an' all that sort of thing,' she said cheerfully. 'Well, now *that's* settled, let's get on, or we'll have to come back before we get there.'

They fell into groups again, and strolled onwards, discussing the School's chances of tennis for the season. Now and again, Jo's quick ear caught the sound of stealthy footsteps near them, for Frau Eisen and her hopeful son could not be described as experienced trackers. But she said nothing, only talked on about games, firmly checking any attempts of the other girls at side-tracking the conversation.

Their path led them through a little wooded shelf, and then out on to bare limestone, where tufts of grass and gentians and edelweiss were the only things growing about the way, and the path was toilsome.

'Those beauties will have to come out into the open now,' she said. 'There's no cover anywhere. Round this boulder, Jack. Now give me your hand. Then when I'm up, you can give the others a boost.'

With the help of his hand she scrambled, more agilely than gracefully, up the boulder. Then, lying at full length along it, she stretched out her hand, and helped to haul up the others. Finally, there was only the doctor himself left standing beneath it.

'Can you manage?' asked Jo. 'I'm afraid you're rather a heavy-weight for me to haul up. It *can* be done alone, for I've done it. But then, I've done a good deal more scrambling than you have."

'Clear out, all of you, and give me the fairway,' he replied.

The girls retreated further up the goat-track that led up at this point, and, getting as far back as he could, he secured a short run which enabled him to leap to a narrow foothold halfway up the boulder. From there, it was child's play for an active young man to find a grip in a little crevice, and lever himself up till he was able to sprawl safely, if inelegantly, across the great rock-mass.

'Ouf! That was a bit of a teaser!' he remarked, producing his handkerchief and dusting his hands and face. 'Is there any more like it, Joey?'

'No; that's the worst bit. And you managed a lot better than I did,' said Jo comfortingly.

'Jo! Is this the only way up?' asked Jeanne in a whisper.

'So far as I know,' replied Jo, lowering her voice. '*Jeanne!* You aren't afraid, surely?'

'I'm—not afraid,' replied Jeanne slowly, 'but it is not nice to think people are following one, and listening to what one says.'

'It isn't—but I doubt if they can get up this. I think they'll wait till we come back, and follow us again, and try to hear what we say. However, we are prepared for that, so it doesn't matter.'

But Jeanne was inclined to be nervy, and she looked as if she thought it mattered very much. 'I do not like it. Is there no other way home, then? I hate being spied on like this!'

'Only round the side. It makes a fairly long walk, and not too easy. And we've Robin to consider,' said Jo, sharply.

Jeanne said no more; but as she went she kept casting glances over her shoulder as if she thought Hermann and his mother might have found some way of flying up the boulder. The others thought no more of it, and laughed and talked gaily.

They soon reached the spot where they were to picnic. The girls sat down with sighs of relief, for they were tired after their walk and the accompanying excitement. Jo unpacked the baskets, and presently they were tackling sandwiches, cakes of cream, chocolate, nuts, and marzipan, fruit, and the flasks of coffee.

'That's better,' said Hilary as she finished her third cake. 'I *was* hungry! Isn't the air up here marvellous, though?'

'Like champagne,' agreed Cornelia, sniffing. 'We're pretty high up, I guess. Is it far to the summit, Jo?'

'About another hour,' said Jo, who was lying flat on the ground in an attitude suggestive of having over-eaten. 'I'm not tackling it this afternoon, Corney, so don't ask me. We'll rest and get over the effects of this spread, and then—we'll attend to business.—What on earth is the matter with you *now*, Jeanne? Seen a ghost, or what?'

Jeanne, who had uttered a low cry, turned a white face on her. 'That boy is just behind that rock—I saw him peep out!' She spoke in rapid French. 'Joey, how did her get up *here*?'

Joey sat up, and looked in the direction to which Jeanne had nodded. 'What a nuisance! His mother must have heaved him up, and must be waiting there for him. I never thought she would do that. She ought not, either,' she added virtuously. 'He's only a little chap— eight or nine, I believe. It's no place for a small boy to be alone.'

'Well, she's done it,' said Hilary desperately. 'What are we to do about—you know what?'

'Do? Play hide-and-seek, of course,' said the doctor calmly. 'Rob, you and Evvy keep together. Can you tuck the precious document into your blazer somewhere? Then get it. Come and pack up, you people—and sur- round her,' he added in a lower tone, for though they were all speaking French, they had no means of knowing whether Hermann understood it or not, and it was foolish to take risks. 'Now, Rob, tuck it away. Does it show? No? Good. Now then, you people, two and two. I'll seek, and you hide. Mind you keep with your partner, and don't go far.'

'Shall I hide it at once?' whispered Robin.

He shook his head. 'No; wait for a turn or two to put that young man off the scent. Now then, be off! I'll give you three minutes to hide, and then I'm coming. This rock is Home.'

They sped off with laughter, even Jeanne beginning to forget her fears, and a very bored small boy, crouched behind a rock, watched them longingly. He had already been sharply scolded for using the Nazi greeting. And then he had been pushed up a rock and bidden keep those 'foreigners' in sight. Now they were scattering, and how could he follow them all? Hermann was only a small boy, after all, and he was very near dissolving

42

into tears. Why couldn't his mother climb the rock and watch the girls herself? Besides, that Herr Doktor was there, and he had once given Hermann a sound beating for throwing stones at a kitten.

Meanwhile, the 'Herr Doktor,' having given the girls the requisite three minutes, was setting out to seek them. He cast a casual glance at the baskets. Apart from Hermann, there was unlikely to be anyone near. They would be safe enough. He left them, and went to hunt.

Hermann had seen the girls packing the remnants of the feast, and he was hungry. He waited a few moments. Then temptation was too much for him. He stole out from his hiding-place, and made for the baskets, with one ear listening for footsteps, and one eye on the place where he had seen girls and doctor disappear.

Luck was on his side. The first basket he searched had three sandwiches and half a dozen cakes in it. The small boy filled his pockets, snatched up a flask standing near, and a fountain-pen someone had dropped, and darted back to his hiding-place just as wild shouts coming nearer told him that someone was returning. So Jo and Jeanne, reaching 'Home' breathless and laughing, with the doctor in full pursuit, missed him. They sat down to chatter while the doctor went to catch someone else, and succeeded, grabbing Hilary by a terrific effort.

Hilary took her turn at seeking, and then Jo herself was seeker. This time, Robin was with Hilary, and when the Head Girl turned to her as they went off with an eager, 'Now, Rob, this is your show. Where shall we hide?' she caught at the outstretched hand.

'My cave,' she whispered. 'Come on, Hilary! Round here—quick!'

CHAPTER VI

'WHERE ARE ROBIN AND HILARY?'

THE doctor was hiding with Evadne, and Cornelia and Jeanne were together. Joey, with a shrewd suspicion as to the whereabouts of the other two, left them till last, once time was up, and started to track down the others. Skirting round a huge boulder a little way down the mountain, she almost fell over Cornelia and Jeanne, who leaped up from their hiding-place and tore off up the slope, Home. Jo could scud with the best but she was rather at a disadvantage, having had to recover her balance, so the pair reached their goal safely, and were sitting fanning themselves with their handkerchiefs when she arrived, panting.

'Ouf! I'm hot!' sighed Jeanne. 'And thirsty, also. Where is the coffee that was left, Joey? May I have some?'

'Rather,' puffed Jo. 'Give me some, too, before I go and hunt up the rest. That purple flask, Jeanne—and the black one near Corney. I think the red one has some in, too.'

Jeanne rooted in the basket for cups, and poured out the coffee. 'We'd better leave some for the others,' she said, sweetening it liberally. 'There you are, Joey.— Corney, here's yours.—You say the black flask is full, Joey? And the red? But I do not see the red.'

'Oh, it'll be there somewhere.' Joey had drained her cup. 'It may have been put back into one of the other baskets. Look for it, Jeanne.'

She went off, and Jeanne and Cornelia, refreshed and growing cooler, amiably rummaged for the red flask. It was not there, and Jeanne looked round. 'It has been set among the tree-roots,' she said. 'You look this side, and I will look that, Corney.'

They parted, to examine the tree-roots for the missing flask, and it was only after a very thorough search that they were sure that the red flask was gone. They came back to the baskets, where the doctor and Evadne were sitting, drinking their share of the coffee, and reported the loss.

'Oh, nonsense!' said the doctor. 'It was here all right— nearly full, too. You haven't looked properly. Here, I'll have a go!'

But though he certainly searched as thoroughly as he could, and all three of the girls helped, the flask did not turn up. Neither, for that matter, did Jo, who had been gone at least ten minutes in search of Hilary and Robin.

At first everyone was too much bothered about the disappearance of a perfectly good flask to bother about the non-appearance of Jo and the other two. But when the doctor, with a sudden feeling that this game was taking rather longer than usual, glanced at his watch, he gave an exclamation. 'Great Peter! Jo's been gone *twenty minutes*! What on earth can she be doing? It's getting on, and I don't want to be caught out on the mountain-side after dark with all you girls. Give her a call, some of you.'

They obeyed; but though they called and cooeed till they were nearly hoarse, they got no answer, and the doctor's face was very grave. It was still early April, and darkness would come down by nineteen or so (for here they used mid-continental time). Already it was half-past sixteen, and they were a good hour and a half's walk from the Sonnalpe. He felt inclined to give Joey a good shaking when he got hold of her.

Meanwhile the others were still hunting, and suddenly Jeanne gave a cry. "Why, Evvy! Here is your fountain-pen! How could it get up here behind this rock? You have not hidden here at all, have you?'

'My fountain-pen?' Evadne clutched at her blazer-pocket. 'So it is! But how *could* it be there? I've never been near the place. This is another mystery, I guess.'

'Do you?' said Cornelia grimly. 'Well, I *don't*—I *know*. That awful boy is up here, isn't he? He's stolen

45

our flask, of course. He could easily do it, for no one stayed to watch the food. You must have dropped the pen some time, Evvy, and he's picked it up. Then he's made off, but dropped the pen—likely through some hole in his pocket, and we've found it. That's *my* guess, and if you've a better, trot it out.'

Jeanne uttered a fresh cry. 'That boy—I had forgotten him! Oh, he has followed Hilary and Robin, and they are caught. Will they take them to the Gestapo?'

'Rubbish!' said the doctor trenchantly, though his eyes were anxious. 'He's only a kid. Hilary alone could handle him easily. But it's quite likely he's followed them, and they are hiding, and not daring to come out in case he finds that precious paper of yours.'

'Then what about Jo?' demanded Evadne, as she safety-pinned her pocket over the restored fountain-pen. 'What's *she* doing?'

'Guess she's treed, too,' said Cornelia cheerfully. 'Well, I suppose we'd better go and find the lot. We'll hand Hermann over to your tender mercies, Dr. Jack,' she added, still cheerfully. 'I don't envy him one mite, either.'

'Do any of you know where the place is?' demanded the doctor, passing over her comments for the time being.

'I have no idea at all,' said Jeanne. 'It was Robin's secret, and neither she nor Jo ever told us *where* it was.'

'Can't you guess, any of you? How long do you think we're likely to stay up here? I don't want to spend the night—and Robin certainly must not. Put your brains in steep, and *think* can't you?'

The three girls looked very serious. The Robin had been so much stronger of late, and they had forgotten the great need of care in her case.

At last, Evadne spoke. 'I think it must be round to the east side of the mountain, for I know they didn't go off to the west or up.'

'Shall we mosey about that way a mite, and see if

we can get the track?' asked Cornelia. 'You go up, Jeanne, with Dr Jack; and Evvy and I will try this way. If Robin found it, I guess *we* can find it somehow. Anyway, we can try—and saints can't do more.'

Her persistent cheerfulness had its effect on them. Jeanne began to climb the mountain track, followed by the doctor, who only paused to shout after the other two, 'If you haven't found anyone in twenty minutes' time, come back here and wait till we come. Mind that, you two!'

But they got no further, any of them, for there came the sound of flying footsteps, and the next minute Jo burst through the bushes. Such a Jo! with white face, black eyes full of fear, her long, thick plaits tumbling over her shoulders, and a huge rent in her skirt.

'Jack!' she cried, and her beautiful voice was hoarse with fear. 'I've been to the cave, and they aren't there! There isn't a sign of them anywhere. But that little Nazi beast was there, and I shook it out of him that he had seen them go in. I told him to come with me—here he is,' she added, as the doctor slipped an arm round her to steady her, for she was shaking with fear. '*Beat* the truth out of him if you must!'

Mercifully for the weeping Hermann who was lagging painfully after the tall girl, there was no need to carry out her ferocious suggestion. He had been crouched down behind the stone just outside the cleft, when a whirlwind had fallen on him from behind.

Up till then, he had been rather inclined to pat himself on the back. As the Head Girl had passed him with her much smaller companion, he had noticed the end of a large packet sticking up from the latter's coat-pocket. He had leaped to the conclusion that this must be some important paper and had promptly tracked the two. He had seen them squeeze through the cleft and at first he had tried to follow them. But soon, frightened by the thick dark, he had turned round, and stumbled out to the opening, where he had decided to hide till they came back. But Jo had upset all his plans, and by the time she had finished with him, Hermann's small tail was well between his legs and he dared do nothing but obey her.

It took the doctor some time to understand all this, sobbed out as it was in Low German. But at length he had got it, and he straightened up with a sigh of relief. 'Then they are in the cave. Thank Heaven for that! Don't look so terrified, Joey darling. We'll soon get them!'

'But you don't understand!' cried Joey. 'I've been into the cave—I went there before I found this little wretch—and they aren't there!'

'They must be! Look here, Jo, how could you go there without a torch?' The doctor spoke urgently.

'It's a fairly straight path. If you go along, and then turn to the right, you come to a kind of cave which is lighted from vent-holes in the roof. I think they must be cracks in the rock-face, covered with scrub. It's like that all the way after that. It's only at first that it's pitch-dark. And it's extra light just now, for the vent-holes lie on the west side—they *must*, from the way the light falls.'

'Is it far in? There are no chasms, or anything like that?'

'Solid floor all the time; and, so far as I know, there's no way out but the one.'

Evadne grabbed the shrinking Hermann by the shoulder. 'Did you see them come out?'

He shook his head dully. 'No, gracious lady. No one came out, but the—the—*her*!' He pointed at Jo, who was still leaning heavily on Jack Maynard's shoulder, for she felt as if her trembling legs would not bear her weight.

'Then they're still there. Probably they heard Hermann, and hid in some cleft or other. Likely they'll be coming along now, for they must have heard Jo if she treated the kid as he says she did. I'll bet he yelled when she got hold of him.'

'He yelled all right,' said Jo shortly. 'Little coward!'

'Well, then, that's what's happened. Hasn't anyone got a torch?'

Jack Maynard fumbled in his pocket, and produced

one. 'Here you are. I had it recharged yesterday, and I haven't used it since.'

'And I have mine, also.' And Jeanne held up a slender pocket torch. 'It is newly charged, and should last. Have we any others?'

They had not; but there were matches in one of the baskets, and both Joey and Jack carried automatic lighters, so they could manage.

'Then come along,' said Cornelia. 'We'll bring the baskets and leave them in the opening to the cave. Then all of us will go and hunt, and we'll soon find them, I guess. Don't look like that, Joey. If we don't meet the pair of 'em coming along, we'll get 'em sooner or later.'

It was the best they could do. They formed up, the two Americans taking Hermann between them, and Jeanne walking at Jo's other side. Of the party, Jo was the most distressed, mentally. But Hermann was almost done. He was only nine, and his experiences of the afternoon had worn him out. Evadne and Cornelia, each gripping him by an arm, marched him forward in grim silence, carrying baskets in their other hands.

At long last they reached the entrance to the cave. There they paused, and Hermann sank to the ground. He could go no longer, as the doctor's experienced eye told him, when he looked over the child. 'He's done,' he said. 'Look here, Jeanne, will you stay with him and the baskets while the rest of us search the cave? He's too tired to give you any trouble. The kid's exhausted. He's dropping off to sleep with weariness. Probably he'll sleep for the next hour or two if he gets the chance.'

Jeanne nodded. 'I will stay with pleasure. I'm tired, too.' She sat down rather limply beside the baskets. Then she took one of the raincoats and spread it carefully over the sleeping child. 'He ought not to sleep uncovered. It is cold, even though the sun is still shining.'

Jack Maynard took up another, and threw it round her. 'Put this on properly. If you're tired, you're likely to be cold as well as Hermann. We'll be as quick as we can, so don't get alarmed.' Then he turned, and led

49

the way in at the narrow cleft, after a struggle to get his broad shoulders through. In the narrow passage, he switched on his powerful torch, lighting the way, and the girls followed, Joey immediately behind, the two Americans in the rear.

In a few minutes, the girls felt that they were climbing upwards. Through cracks and clefts in the rock roof came rifts of light, and Jack Maynard extinguished his torch. They had come to the little cave Jo had spoken of. Now she led the way straight across it to another passage, which still mounted steadily. The way was rocky but it was dry enough, and the golden evening light pouring down made it more cheerful than it might have been. They could feel a fresh breeze blowing, and Dr Jack reflected that it ought not to be hard for a practised mountaineer to find more than one way out if necessary. Then the light vanished, and he hastily switched on his torch again.

They had left the passage, and were standing in a cave of good size. It was by no means enormous; but it was not small. It must have been over a hundred feet wide, and about a third as long again. At one end was a heap of stones, almost like a cairn, with a large, flat stone on the top. But it was empty. There was no one there but themselves, and, for the first time in this expedition, Dr Jack felt his heart sink, as he passed quickly round the place lighting up every smallest chink or cranny.

At length he returned to Jo and the girls, who were standing quietly at the entrance to the inner cave where he had left them. 'It's most mysterious, but they certainly aren't here.—Now don't faint, Joey!' he added quickly, his arm going round her again as she swayed dangerously. 'They may have come out while you were herding Hermann to us, and have taken another way to our picnic place. It's quite likely. Our best plan, I think, is to go back, and wait a little. If they don't come, then we must get back to the Sonnalpe, and have search-parties sent out. But I don't believe it'll be necessary. Come along, dear. Lean on me. You're worn out, what with the walk, and the game, and this worry.'

'The paper!' exclaimed Cornelia urgently. 'Rob was to hide it here. We can't leave it now, Dr Jack. Everyone will know about this place before long. We must find it, and take it back with us. It'll have to go somewhere else.'

'Good thought, Corney! No; we certainly can't leave a thing like that here. Jo, have you any idea where Rob meant to put it?'

'In the niche in that altar-arrangement,' said Joey. She led the way to the cairn. 'See; down here. There's just a tiny place. Rob and I thought it would be quite safe. We only found the way here by accident, when we were out this way one day. Feel for the paper, Evvy. It'll be well in.'

Evadne felt, and poked to some purpose, but her search was fruitless. There was no paper there. They all tried, the doctor flashing his light about. Plainly, wherever the paper was, it was not in the cairn. Jo's eyes were full of dumb despair as she lifted them to Jack Maynard's face. 'Jack! What does it mean? Have they gone? Or have they never been there?'

'Never been there, I should think,' said Evadne. 'Well, *would* Robin be likely to hide the thing there when she knew that she was followed? And she must have known. Hermann wouldn't move like a young fawn, I guess.'

'Then—then—oh, *where* are Robin and Hilary? Jack, I can't bear it!' And half-fainting, Jo collapsed in the strong arms holding her, with tearless sobs.

CHAPTER VII

A SHOCK FOR JOEY—AND MADGE

WHEN Hilary and Robin ran off across the shoulder of the mountain, they had quite forgotten that Hermann Eisen was near by. The interest of the game, and the thrill of hiding the precious document, had seized on them to the exclusion of everything else.

'Round here, Hilary!' panted Robin, when they reached the edge of the trees. 'Now across here. Hurry! We must be quick, for I do not wish to be found in the cave, and it will take a few minutes to reach the place Joey and I have thought of.'

'We can't break our necks,' said Hilary sensibly. 'Besides, Jo is fairly sure to have guessed, and she'll hunt the others first.'

So they slowed down, greatly to the relief of Hermann, who was unable to run as they did, firstly because his legs were too short, and secondly because there was very little cover here, and he knew that if the girls saw him, his game would be ended. They struck across a little plateau of bare limestone, round a curve, and so reached a spot where coarse grass and low shrubs gave their tracker some cover, though not much. Then they turned to the rock wall, and here Hermann rubbed his eyes and blinked, for the Robin literally disappeared into it. However, Hilary, much more sturdily built, did not find it so easy, and he was able to creep up fairly close, and note the spot.

Hermann waited till he thought the girls must be well inside, and then followed. While bigger in build than Robin, who was very small and slight for her years, he had no difficulty in entering. Just ahead of him, he saw a pale, dancing light and guessed it to be a torch. Setting his teeth, he followed, for he dared do nothing else. His mother had taught him that all such work as this was done for the Führer, and would be specially blessed. Hermann was no braver than the majority of small boys, but he nerved himself to go forward. At least he knew that the girls were there, and they had a light. Then, just as he was beginning to feel a little braver, the light vanished, and the sound of the girls' steps and their voices ceased. He was alone in thick darkness, which seemed to press heavily down on him. He could not know that his last stumble had reached Hilary's quick ears, nor that she had said urgently, 'Robin! Stop a minute! I think we're being followed!'

Robin obediently stopped, and, in the silence that
52

followed, they heard Hermann's footsteps, as he fumbled his way down the narrow passage. Hilary had switched off her torch as she spoke, and she stood with her arm round Robin's shoulders, both of them almost afraid to breathe lest they should be heard.

There was a little interval. Then they heard the stumbling footsteps stop, turn, and go the other way. Still keeping an arm round the younger girl, Hilary gently pushed her on in the way they had been going. Robin understood, and led the way. Presently, they reached the part lighted through the rifts in the mountain-side, and here it was easier. Neither spoke, however, for though they could hear no one following them, they could not be certain that they were safe. Indeed, it was not until they stood in the inner cave, the beam from Hilary's torch just giving them a faint idea of the size, that they dared to speak.

'Where did you think of putting the paper?' asked Hilary in an undertone.

'In the stone heap over there,' said Robin, pointing to the cairn at the far side. 'There is a tiny crevice, and Jo and I thought it would be a very safe hiding-place. What do you think, Hilary?'

Hilary mused for a moment. 'It probably would have been,' she said at length, 'but not now, Rob. Whoever was after us—and I'll bet it was that sickening small boy —knows of this place. He could easily show someone the way here, and they'd soon pull down that heap of stones and find our vow. I'm sure the Nazis would make a fearful fuss about even a schoolgirls' affair.'

'Well, what are we to do, then?' asked Robin. 'Take it back with us? But then how shall we keep it safe?'

'We *must* take it back with us,' said Hilary. 'Can you bear the darkness a little, Rob? If so, I'll switch this thing off. It's newly charged, but it would be a pity to use it unnecessarily, when we may need it rather badly later on.'

'Why? What do you mean?' asked Robin in some surprise.

'Well, whoever was following us seems to have given

that up; but I'm fairly certain he'll be sitting at the mouth of this place, waiting to catch us. In that case, the list is unsafer than ever. So I want to see if we can possibly find another way out.'

'I don't think there is one. Joey and I looked, but we couldn't find one,' objected Robin.

'Quite likely. But then it wasn't a case of have-to. This is. Now, Robin, you get behind those stones, and stay there. I'm going to explore and see what I can find.' And Hilary, having ensconced the younger girl safely behind the cairn, set off on her voyage of discovery.

At first it seemed as if she were doomed to disappointment. Then an idea struck her. Raising her torch, she played the light on the upper part of the walls, and after making nearly the entire circuit of the cave, she found her persistence rewarded. Well above her head was a cleft. Hilary believed it might lead out to the mountainside. She resolved to try. Calling softly, she summoned the Robin to her side, and then bade her get on to her shoulders.

'Can you hold me?' asked the Robin doubtfully.

Hilary laughed. 'Hold two of you, kiddy. On to my back! Now, get to my shoulders. Right? Then take the torch and see if you can flash it round that cleft. I'll steady you. Carefully, now. We don't want an accident in this hole. 'The Robin was careful. She was just able to reach up, and see into the cleft. She uttered a low cry of delight. 'Hilary! It's another passage like the one leading in here. There are holes through which the light comes. Can you stand firm? I am going to jump.'

'Robin! You are not to go far from here,' cried Hilary in sudden alarm. 'We don't know where this path may lead, and we have no string with us. Promise me not to go far, or I'll move.'

'I'm just going a very little way,' said the Robin soothingly.

And she jumped, nearly sending Hilary to her knees. However, the elder girl, by a huge effort, contrived to keep on her feet, and looking up to where she could see the pale torch-light flickering, she called up anxiously, 'Rob! Are you all right? What is it like?'

'Ever so much lighter,' reported Robin, appearing in the opening with stunning suddenness. 'Can you get up, Hilary? I believe we can get out this way. There must be a big hole somewhere, and it faces to the west, for the sunset light is pouring in.'

Hilary looked round for inspiration. There was nothing in the cave to help her. Then she had an idea. 'Rob! I'm going to toss up the girdle from my frock. See if you can find a knob at either side of the opening to fasten it—clove-hitch knots, mind. Then I'll jump, and if it holds I think I can haul myself up. Are there any knobs?'

The Robin turned the light on either side. 'One here,' she said. 'Oh, yes! And one just a little higher up here. It will not be straight. Will that matter? It is not much.'

'So long as it isn't *too* squint! Here you are; catch!' And Hilary tossed up the little bundle with a direct aim that spoke well for her cricket. The Robin caught it. Luckily, it was a stitched girdle and long, and she easily fastened it across the opening, making it secure with clove-hitch knots which, like most Guides, she knew well enough to make in the dark. When it was secure, she stood back. 'It's ready, Hilary. Can you manage?'

'I've got to,' said Hilary stubbornly, as she took several steps back to get a clear run. 'Shine the light on it, Rob, so that I have some idea where to grab. Now then! I'm coming!' And she set off at her hardest pace, finishing with a high jump that just enabled her to clutch the frail bar with one hand, while with the other she grabbed at the limestone side of the passage, luckily encountering a tiny projection which she gripped firmly. Mercifully, both withstood the strain by a miracle —for limestone can often be very rotten. With a complicated muscular effort, she levered herself up, and reached the place just as Joey was entering the lower passage for the first time. This, however, the daring pair did not know, and they removed Hilary's girdle, and then set off down this new place, with hearts full of hope, for the Robin had spoken truly when she said it was much lighter than any of the rest.

'I should think we haven't much further to go, Rob,' Hilary said when half an hour's steady walking had brought them to a place where the light seemed even stronger, and the air fresher.

Robin chuckled. 'If whoever chased us up the first passage waits till we come out again, he will have a long time to wait, n'est-ce pas?'

Hilary glanced down at her. She knew quite well that Joey would never be content to wait till they returned. Whoever was lying in ambush was quite likely to be discovered; and, if Hilary knew her Jo, none too gently. However, Robin had plainly not thought of it, and the Head Girl hesitated at the thought of reminding her what Jo's frenzy would be like. The two were devoted to each other, and Robin would be quite likely to insist on going back if she thought Jo would suffer.

At this point, Robin gave a little squeal, and suddenly darted forward. 'Hilary! If we can get through this bush, we can get out! See! It is quite big. But the bush is in the way—the hole, I mean,' she added incoherently. 'Oh, can we manage it?'

Hilary felt in her blazer-pocket, and produced the big Scout knife without which she rarely moved. 'Out of the way, my child! We'll soon manage *this*.'

'Do not cut more than you can help, lest others should find the path,' suggested the Robin. 'It may be useful yet. Cut carefully.'

'I'll be careful,' agreed Hilary. 'Just this chunk, I think. Then we can wriggle through. Mercifully, it doesn't mean such a terrific leap as getting up to this place was. Now then, Rob, clear out of the way. I'm going up.'

Ten minutes later, scratched, untidy, with their hair truly looking as if they had been 'dragged through a hedge backwards,' and their frocks badly torn, the pair stood out on the mountain slope in time to see the sun set behind the great limestone ridges on the opposite side of the Tiern See in a glory of rose and saffron.

'We can't stop a minute!' cried Hilary, grabbing

Robin's hand. 'It will be dark in no time, and I haven't the faintest idea where we are.'

'I have, though,' said the Robin. 'We are just about ten minutes from the summit, and it is a straight path down to the Sonnalpe. Also, Hilary, it will be a starry night, and the moon rises early. We shall be quite safe. But had we not better return to the picnic place?'

'No; straight home is our best bet,' declared Hilary, hurrying her down the path at top speed. 'Don't talk, Rob! Keep your breath for our journey. You'll need it.'

Robin would have liked to protest, for now she was awaking to the fact that Jo would be horribly worried when neither she nor Hilary appeared in the cave. But Hilary was pressing downwards at a pace that nearly robbed her of her breath, and she could only go whither the Head Girl pulled her. Down, down, down! Robin began to think they would never get there. Then, suddenly, they saw the twinkling lights of a car, and a familiar voice said, 'Hilary! And our Vögelein! What are you doing out here at this hour?'

'Gottfried!' cried the Robin. 'Oh, but I am glad to see thee! We have been having a picnic, and Hilary and I were separated from the rest, and Hilary *would* come down instead of going to seek them.'

'That is good,' said Dr Mensch, stowing them into his car. 'Now we will have you both home speedily. Have the others reached school yet?'

'I've no idea,' said Hilary. 'I shouldn't think so. But if *we* go back to school, someone could take the car and go to meet them. I knew Rob mustn't be out in the night-air, so I just hustled her back.'

'And were quite right,' smiled the young doctor. 'Our Blümchen is not a night-blooming flower. She is best in the house then.'

Five minutes later, he had decanted Hilary at the school gates and was running on to Die Rosen, where he handed Robin over to a startled Madge who, when she heard the story, packed her charge off to bed after a hot bath and a jorum of boiling milk and rolls and butter.

So it was that, when a distraught Jo was nearly carried

into the house by Jack Maynard two hours later, she was greeted with the news that the Robin was fast asleep in her own bed.

The shock was too much for Joey. She gave a funny little gasp, and would have fallen, but for the young doctor's arm which was still encircling her. He lifted her, laid her on a couch, and speedily brought her round. Jo came to herself, to find that she was lying on the settee in the salon at Die Rosen, with Madge hovering anxiously round, and Jack Maynard holding her closely to him. For no particular reason she buried her head on his shoulder, and began to weep even more bitterly than a terrified Hermann was doing at the other side of the room.

Madge would have tried to console her; but Jack Maynard gave *her* a shock. Holding Joey very tightly to him, he said in tones there was no mistaking, 'Never mind, my darling. It's all over, and Robin is safe. Just cry it all out and you'll feel better.'

And before the stunned Madge could gasp out any ejaculation, Joey sobbed, 'Oh, Jack—what a—solid lump—of comfort you—are!'

After that, as Madge told her husband later on, the only thing she could do was to leave the room, taking weary Hermann with her, and wait with what patience she could assume for a full account of the story when, to quote herself, 'Jack and Jo should have come to their common or garden senses.'

CHAPTER VIII

THE GESTAPO

'JOEY *engaged*! Engaged to be married, you mean? I don't believe it! It's a have!' And Miss Cochrane, better known to readers of former chronicles of the Chalet School as Grizel, uttered a scornful laugh.

The Robin, who had just given her the great news,

flushed. 'But it *is* true. She and Jack have been engaged for nearly a month now.'

'Impossible!' declared Grizel. 'Why, she's always laughed at that sort of thing, and said she would never marry. I don't believe even Jack Maynard could make her change her mind. It's a mistake.'

'It *isn't*,' insisted the Robin, who had begged to be allowed to be the one to tell Grizel Cochrane and Juliet Carrick, now Juliet O'Hara. 'That night we had the picnic up the Sonnenscheinspitze they were engaged; but Joey asked us not to tell anyone till after the holidays, as Juliet's wedding was coming, and she did not want to spoil the excitement for her. Jack gave her her ring the day the School broke up. She would not have it before, lest anyone should see it and guess.'

Grizel collapsed into the nearest chair. 'You've taken my breath away,' she said limply. 'It's the *last* thing I should have expected Jo to do.' Then she sat up again. 'Break the news gently, Rob. When are they to be married?'

'Jack wishes to have it soon,' said Robin, balancing on an arm of the settee. 'If we have trouble with the Nazis, he says that Jem must look after Madge and the children. He wants the right to look after Jo—and me,' she added as an afterthought.

'Yes,' said Grizel. 'I suppose whoever takes Joey will have to take you as well. Poor Jack Maynard!' she ended with a slight frown. Grizel Cochrane had always been jealous of Jo's love for her little adopted sister. But she had a deep affection for Madge Russell and Joey, and, as she was inclined to be possessive, disliked the idea that Jo, especially, should care more for anyone than herself.

Joey, deeply interested in other folk, with a heart as wide as the world, would never have submitted to such an exclusive friendship, as others than Grizel had found, and the elder sister had been careful to say nothing. But Grizel had always resented the Robin.

Now, she said lightly, '*Your* nose will be out of joint now, my dear.'

'Why should it be?' asked the Robin, opening wide eyes, and feeling her pretty little nose carefully. 'It is quite all right, Grizel.'

'I meant,' said Grizel, 'that your place is taken. You aren't first with Joey now. How d'you like having to play second fiddle?'

The Robin's eyes flashed. 'I don't! Joey loves me just as much as she ever did. It's *different!*'

Grizel opened her lips to say something else. But the gallant little figure somehow made her ashamed of herself, and she laughed instead. 'I expect it is. Oh, Joey will always have room and time for you, baby. But your news is simply stunning. I *can't* believe it! Jo engaged to be married!'

'Well, here comes Joey herself, so perhaps you can believe it when you see *her*,'' suggested the Robin coldly, jumping to the floor.

The door opened, and Jo herself entered, an unusual flush on her cheeks, but her head held high. She was rather afraid of Grizel's comments, but not for worlds would she have let her know.

'Hello, Joey! Come here and tell me if you've put Robin up to this amazing story of hers,' said Grizel, advancing to kiss her friend.

'As I don't know exactly what Robin may have been telling you, I'm afraid I can't say offhand,' replied Jo, returning the kiss.

For answer, Grizel caught at her left hand, lifted it, and looked in silence at the big emerald blazing on the fourth finger. Jo blushed deeper, and her long lashes fell on her cheeks as the elder girl dropped the hand and took her by the shoulders.

'So it is really true, Joey? I simply couldn't believe it, you know. After all you've said——'

Jo laughed in embarrassed fashion. 'I know. But that was when I was young and silly.' She lifted her eyes, and looked straight into the grey ones on a level with her own. 'Won't you wish me happiness, Grizel? You're my oldest friend, you know.'

Again ashamed of herself, Grizel pressed forward for

another kiss. 'Of course I do. May you be very happy indeed, Joey dear. You deserve it, if ever a girl did. I hope you'll always find life good.'

'Oh, well, that's too much to hope, I'm afraid,' said Jo gently. 'Thank you, Grizel. I know you mean it. And you must come to the wedding, dear, and be one of my maids, too. Will you?'

'*Chief* bridesmaid? Oh, Joey, I'd love it!'

Joey shook her head. 'Only a sister could be chief bridesmaid. Rob will be that. But I want you to pair with Frieda—if she can come. She may not, of course. Jem won't say yet if he thinks I ought to ask her. She's safe where she is. It may not be best for her to come.'

As if in answer to her doubt, there came a thundering knock at the hall-door, and two minutes later, Marie, wife of André le Mesurier, Jem Russell's servant and housekeeper at Die Rosen, appeared, looking frightened. 'Mamzelle, there is a man here who wishes to speak with you and Mamzelle Robin. Shall I bring him in?'

'A man?' said Joey, puzzled. 'Who is it? Did he give no name?'

But the visitor showed himself at this moment. 'The Fräulein Josephine Bettany?' he queried, reading from a paper he carried.

Jo swung round on him indignantly. 'I do not know you, mein Herr, but I am Fräulein Bettany. What do you want with me?'

'I am from the Gestapo, and I have orders to take you to Innsbruck to answer questions there before the judicial court,' he replied.

'*What?*' Joey stared at him in amazement. 'What sort of questions?'

'Das Fräulein will doubtless learn that when she reaches the court.'

'Well, I'm not coming. I'm not an Austrian, nor a German, and you have no right to force your way in here!' Joey's clear tones rose, and reached her sister's ears as she came down the stairs, small Sybil clinging to her hand.

61

The man shrugged his shoulders. 'However, there is now no Austria. All is the great Reich, and you have offended against the laws of the Reich. You must answer for it, mein Fräulein, as all must.'

Releasing her hand, Madge said sharply, 'Sybil, go back upstairs, and tell Rosa that you are all to stay in the nursery—at once!'

Startled by her mother's peremptory tone, for Madge never spoke anything but gently to the children unless they were naughty, Sybil turned at once and stumped off upstairs, while Mrs Russell marched into the salon to find her young sister facing a German with flaming cheeks and flashing eyes.

'What is all this?' demanded the mistress of the house.

The man turned to her with an insolent gesture. 'The Fräulein is commanded to return with me to Innsbruck and answer questions at the Court of Justice,' he replied. 'She refuses to go. But she must understand, meine Frau, as you must also, that she is not in a position to refuse.'

'Miss Bettany is a British subject, and not amenable to such treatment,' retorted Madge. 'Nor will my husband permit it. Grizel—ah, here he is. Now, mein Herr, you will be answered,' as the doctor came in through the open French window.

'What on earth is wrong?' he inquired, looking round at the excited little group.

The man enlightened him with a shade more respect in his tones. He had not realised that Miss Bettany might be under the protection of anyone so powerful as the great doctor of the Sonnalpe Sanatorium, and he moderated his demands a little. Jem heard him out in silence.

'Let me see that order,' he said when the policeman had done.

The man handed it over, and Jem scanned it. 'There is no reason given here for your attempted apprehension of Miss Bettany. Of what is she accused?'

'Of espionage against the Great Reich,' was the reply.

'Indeed? And why? Who has accused her?'

'You must know, Herr Doktor, that I know nothing

of that. My orders are to bring her to Innsbruck,' said the man civilly.

'And the Fräulein Robin Humphries is included here, I see. Also Hilary Burn, Evadne Lannis, Cornelia Flower, and Jeanne le Cadoulec. You know, I suppose, that the last-named is French, and die Fräulein Lannis and Flower are American. It would be well, I think, if you interviewed the various consuls, first. However, we can easily settle the question of the British girls. Our consul is up here, paying a visit to a friend of his. I will have him rung up, and he shall come along and answer you. I am certain that you will not be permitted to interfere with the girls in any way. I know that your Government wants no international entanglements at present.—Grizel!' He turned to Grizel. 'Go and ring up the Sanatorium, and ask if Mr Hanson can come at once.'

Grizel went at once. Meanwhile, Joey turned on the man. 'One moment! Who else is included in this precious accusation?'

'That is——' began the man insolently. Then he caught Jem's eye and wilted. 'There is one of the doctors, mein Fräulein—the Herr Doktor Maynard.'

'I *thought* so!' said Joey emphatically. 'All this, I suppose, comes from Frau Eisen. It's a pity if we can't play a harmless game of hide-and-seek without being accused of espionage on the evidence of a woman and a small boy!'

'Hush, Joey,' said Jem sternly. 'There is no need for you to say anything. I will see to all this. As for Maynard, he is under the protection of the British flag here.'

'He's more than that,' announced Grizel, strolling into the room. 'Mr Hanson was in the office, talking to Rosalie, so I told him his presence was required here, and got on to Wien. And here *is* Mr Hanson,' she concluded triumphantly.

Mr Hanson, a quiet, middle-aged Englishman, soon settled the agent of the Gestapo, referring him to the fathers of the two American girls, and to the Comte le Cadoulec, who was also at the Sonnalpe. As Mr Flower and Mr Lannis were millionaires, and able to pull wires

63

in half a dozen departments, while the Comte le Cadoulec was a member of the French Government, the man soon realised that he was up against forces too strong for him so far as the girls were concerned. But Jack Maynard had to go with him. Moreover, Mr Hanson privately warned Madge and Jem that the School would almost certainly have to be closed sooner or later.

'You can't keep on a school in an atmosphere of suspicion,' he said. 'Parents wouldn't allow it. I shouldn't like any child of mine to be out here just now. If I were you, I would make arrangements to close it, or else to move it elsewhere. As for the Sanatorium, Russell, they may try to force you to give it up to German control. The Nazis are determined to hold every post of importance in the land. The Gestapo have a complete stranglehold on the country, and they're going to see to it that only German Nazis benefit by this Anschluss.'

'But, they can't accuse children of espionage!' protested Madge.

'They're capable of anything. I tell you, Russell, no one is safe—except Hitler, and perhaps Göring. And at that, I doubt whether even he is safe if that maniac gets it into his head that Göring wants the command.'

He departed after that, leaving two very serious people behind him.

'I'm afraid he's right, Madge,' said Jem at length. 'The School must be closed. We can't accept the responsibility of having either the girls or the Staff rushed off to their so-called "preventive detention" at any moment.'

Madge was almost in tears. 'It's *my* School, Jem. I built it up from nothing, and though it's I who say it, it's a good School. Must I finish it just because a set of men have gone quite mad?'

'Well, it's either that or move it,' he replied. 'In any case, my dear, I'm going to get you and the children out of this. If I send my own children and my nieces and nephews out of the country, I can't let you keep other people's children here. As for Jack, Hanson will soon get him released. Hitler and Co. want no trouble with the British Empire at present. But in the meantime, the girls can't suffer. And the School is leaving us already, dear. We had over two hundred girls last term. This term there are only a hundred and thirty. I'm sending Margot and her two away at half-term. She's in no case to stand any extra trouble, poor girl!' He frowned as he thought of his only sister, widowed tragically in Australia after her three little sons had died, and now at the Chalet School as one of the matrons. When Margot Venables had reached the Sonnalpe, she had almost gone under with the heavy strain of all she had suffered. The doctor knew that his sister, though apparently well enough now, had very little reserve strength with which to meet fresh demands.

Madge dried her eyes. 'Do you think we could move the School? But then, what about the San? Mr Hanson said they might try to oust you.'

He nodded. 'I'm expecting it at any moment. Look here, Madge, we had better call a meeting of both Staffs, and discuss this with them. But Margot goes at the end of next week, and takes all the children with her. That's settled. Rosalie Dene,' he spoke of his secretary, an old girl of the Chalet School, 'can go with them. Canon Dene wrote to me a few days ago, and he wants Rosalie to go home.'

'Where are you sending them? Oh, Jem, I *don't* want to part with any of them. And Sybil is still just a baby.'

'Mollie and Dick have had to part with four of theirs. This place doesn't seem to be much more healthy than India as things are now. As for where they're going, do you remember that child we had here for a broken ankle, who came from Guernsey? The name was Le Pelley—Jacqueline Le Pelley.'

'I remember her,' said Madge, smiling involuntarily. 'She was a saintly-looking child, rather like a dark Alixe von Elsen, and as full of mischief as she could be. Rather a nice child, I thought.'

'Well, when Germany marched in, I knew that we must send Dick's kids out of the country, whatever we did about our own, so I wrote to her people, and they've taken a house in my name, not far from them.

I'm sending Margot and the children there. I wish you'd make up your mind to part with David and Sybil, too. I don't like their being here.'

Madge sat ruminating for a few minutes. Then she looked up. 'Jem! How would it be if we took the School to Guernsey? And the San, too? I've always heard that the climate is wonderful there. Of course, it wouldn't be mountain air; but it might be as good. What do you say?'

'The School, certainly,' he said heartily. 'We'll think about the San later. And now, dearest, it's getting very late, and you're worn out with all the worry. Let's go to bed. I'll summon that meeting for tomorrow night.'

CHAPTER IX

A NAZI 'SPORT'

THE meeting was duly held next day, and the Staff of the School were all agreed that they must remove to some safer spot, though it went very much against the grain to do so.

'All the same,' said Miss Annersley seriously, 'Dr Jem is right. If we stay here, the School will leave us.'

Frau Mieders shook her head. 'You must go. But I—I fear—must stay. If I could but get little Lieserl away! But they would never permit it. Lieserl is but eighteen. They will insist that she stays here.'

'I come,' said Herr Anserl abruptly. 'I love my country, but I will not stay to see her disgraced by secret imprisonments, maltreating of Jews and concentration camps. If I must escape I must escape. That is all of it. And you, Laubach?'

Herr Laubach shook his head sadly. 'I must stay. My poor wife could not move, so I must just stay. We can but die together.'

Mademoiselle Berné and Mademoiselle Lachenais both declared their intention of going with the School.

'I would not stay here alone—I,' said Mademoiselle Lachenais. 'As you propose to begin again in les Iles Normandes, it will fit very well, for my parents have a summer home in Normandy, so I shall be able to see them often. Doubtless, Madame, when those parents who have withdrawn their children because we are here learn whither we are gone, they will return the girls.'

'But not the German or Austrian girls,' said Madge with a sigh. 'Alixe von Elsen, the Rincinis, the Müllers, Emmie and Joanna Linders—oh, and about fifty others are lost to us—for the next few years, at any rate.'

'What about Dr Jack?' demanded Miss Stewart suddenly. 'Is he back?'

'Not yet,' said Mrs Russell. 'And they have ordered Bruno von Ahlen away, and Gottfried is afraid he must go, too. They say they are sending us other doctors in their place.'

'Spies for the Gestapo,' said Miss Nalder, the Games Mistress.

'Almost certainly,' agreed Jem. 'However, it's a question if we can hold on or not. If things get too bad, we may have to move the Sanatorium too.'

'Won't that be a big loss for you?' asked Miss Wilson abruptly.

'Not so very. For one thing, I countermanded orders for a great deal of new apparatus at the time of the march-in. For another, I have sold the old Chalet buildings and grounds—to Mr Flower. So we are recouped for that loss. All our investments have been changed for safe ones.'

'That's all to the good. But are the Flowers staying on, then?'

'Mr Flower is. But if we move, Cornelia comes with us. He was on the 'phone to me this morning.'

'Well, then, I suppose we had better begin to pack up at once.' Miss Annersley looked round her colleagues at the table, and they all nodded agreement.

The meeting closed on that note, and the Sanatorium also began to prepare, and for the next few days events moved quietly, Jack Maynard returning from Innsbruck at the end of a week in a state of furious indignation over his detention. Jem warned him to keep quiet about it. The Gestapo were convinced that there had been something behind that seemingly innocent game of hide-and-seek, and the English doctor had been released only by strenuous efforts on the part of the British representatives.

'In fact,' concluded Jem, 'if you'll take my advice, you'll marry Jo out of hand, and take her and Robin out of this country. You and Jo can take a honeymoon in France, and be ready to welcome us when we all come.'

Jack Maynard was only too ready to agree. And Joey, after a little, was persuaded to it, though, as she said, she had had no idea of being married for at least a year.

But though the elders might plan wisely, they had reckoned without the younger members of the affair. Their careful arrangements were all brought to naught by a crashing stroke, and nine of them, at least, came in for an adventure that might be thrilling to look back upon, but was sufficiently unpleasant at the time.

It began with a party going down to Spärtz for shopping. Miss Wilson went with them and Joey and Robin joined the party at the last moment. The others were Maria Marani, Jeanne le Cadoulec, Evadne and Cornelia, Robin's chum, Lorenz Maïco, a fourteen-year-old from Hungary, and Margot Venables' elder girl, Daisy, a wide-eyed, yellow-headed irresponsible of twelve. Daisy was to set out for England with her mother and the rest of the Sonnalpe nursery party next day, and she wanted to buy one or two oddments as remembrances for her chums.

They did their shopping in safety. Miss Wilson saw to it that nobody made rude remarks about anything they might see, and by sixteen o'clock they were all in the Gasthaus, drinking coffee and eating cakes ·and fancy-bread twists with good appetite.

Suddenly, as they sat in the window, enjoying the meal and watching what went past, there arose a chorus of yells, hoots, and brutal laughter.

'What on earth's going on?' exclaimed Jo, rising to look over Evadne's fair curls.

Down the side street there came an old man with a long, grey beard, plainly running for his life. A shower of stones, rotten fruit and other missiles followed him. Stark terror was in his face, and already he was failing to outdistance his pursuers.

'Why, that's old Herr Goldmann, the jeweller!' cried Jo. She knew the old Jew well, for he usually had her watch for repairs at least once in two months. He was a decent old soul, kindly, charitable, and honest. 'What are they doing to him? The brutes! *Rob!* What are you after? Come back at once! Oh, my hat!'

For Robin, leaping up from her seat with an energy which overturned her coffee, had fled from the room and the Gasthaus, and was out in the square, making for the old man with all the speed she could. Naturally Jo went after her; and, equally naturally, the other girls followed. The result was that, when the aghast Miss Wilson reached the door, she saw her charges surrounding the terrified old man, Robin with her arms round him, while Jo was haranguing the pursuers with all the strength of her vocabulary, which was considerable.

'You low cads! You cowards!' she cried. 'How dare you chase an old man like this? Twenty of you against one! You—you *huns*! You—Hans Bocher!' she added, catching sight of one young hooligan whom she knew. 'Last winter, when you were all starving, didn't Frau Goldmann send soup and coffee every day to your home? And didn't Herr Goldmann give you a job so that you had a regular wage? And is this the way you show your gratitude? You *deserve* to starve!'

'He's a Jew! Jews have no right to live!' declared Hans Bocher sullenly. 'Give place, Fräulein Bettany, and hand over the old Jew to us! Better take care, or you'll be in trouble for this.'

Cornelia Flower took up the tale. She was so angry that she forgot her German, and spoke in English—or rather, American—which was just as well, since none of them could understand her, though the trend of her speech was unmistakable. Before her flood of language, the young ruffians fell back a moment, and Miss Wilson took advantage of it to drag Robin and Herr Goldmann into the Gasthaus, where she was met by a frightened landlord, who, nevertheless, agreed to put Herr Goldmann through into a courtyard at the back, by which, it was hoped, he might get safely back to his house.

But if Robin was safe, it was more than the other girls were. Already a crowd was collecting, and it was plain that something must be done quickly. As for Robin and Jo, Miss Wilson determined that they must be got out of the country that night if it were possible. Only the facts that Spärtz was a very small town and that they themselves were well known and under powerful protection, kept them free from arrest so far. She must get them away at once before a regular riot arose.

Thrusting the Robin into the arms of the innkeeper, she hastily begged him to get her up to the Sonnalpe at once, and then, without waiting to hear whether he would or not, she plunged out into the throng and fought her way through it till she was behind the girls.

By this time, Jo had succeeded in regaining a little sanity and in hushing Cornelia. In one way, the packed crowd had saved the girls from serious trouble, for the hooligans were too closely hemmed in to throw stones. They stood shoulder to shoulder, a gallant little band, now becoming rather frightened as they heard the low, bestial growl of an enraged populace.

Suddenly Miss Wilson felt a gentle plucking at her sleeve. Turning her head, she saw the parish priest, who knew the School well. He was motioning with his head towards the church that stood at the corner, much nearer where they were than the Gasthaus. Miss Wilson guessed at once what he meant. The church, built in the days of the robber barons to withstand a siege, had a great, nail-studded door, and the windows were small and heavily barred. Once the girls were in there, they were safe for the moment. It might be possible to get them away and up the mountain path before the angry crowd could break in. She hesitated not a moment. Grabbing the

70

shoulder of Jeanne, who was nearest, she said sternly, 'Follow me at once, all of you. Don't dare do anything else!' And began to fight her way through the packed throng.

It was a good thing that she was big and muscular, for it took her all her time to do it, and by the time she had reached the church porch her coat was torn off her back, her hat gone, and her magnificent hair tumbling in curly masses over her shoulders. Jeanne came next; then Hilary. The others clung after them, Joey last, and the priest had slipped eel-like through the crowd, and in at his presbytery, hurrying through the sacristy to open the door. He did it with such suddenness, that Miss Wilson, Jeanne, and Daisy fell forwards into the church. The others followed pell-mell, almost before the mob had realised what was happening.

'Quick!' gasped the priest. 'Help me bar the door!'

Jo and the American girls helped him, and they slammed it shut just in time. They were safe for the moment.

But it was only for the moment, and no one knew this better than Vater Johann. He did not wait, but simply turned, beckoning, and led the way up the centre aisle and into the sanctuary and round the altar. Here he bent and fumbled, and then a door opened, showing the wide, cupboard-like space where were stored the belongings of the Christmas Crib, various pedestals, and sundry other church possessions. Pushing aside the straw used for the Crib, Vater Johann scrambled on all-fours under the altar itself, and fumbled again. This time, a trapdoor lifted, showing, by the tiny electric light he had switched on, a flight of stone steps.

'Down there,' he said, pointing. 'Then straight on till you come out on the mountain-side. I must go back and remove the Blessed Sacrament, and put it in safety. Hasten!'

The urgency with which he spoke put wings to their feet. One by one they entered, and went down the stairs. As Joey's black head, looking wilder than ever before, disappeared, he slammed the trap to, with a fervent blessing on them, and went back into the church to remove its greatest treasure, the Blessed Sacrament, to a place of safety from the disappointed fury of the mob, for well he knew that once they broke in, he need expect no mercy.

Meanwhile, hurrying as fast as they could, the little party went down what seemed to them endless steps. They reached a passage, muddy and smelling of mould, and walked on it for a long way. Miss Wilson noted that for some distance the path ran level. Then it began steadily to ascend, and she felt that before long they would come out on the mountain slope. She hoped that they would come out on the further path. Otherwise, they must go across the water-meadows at Seespitz, and would be plain to the sight of all. She thought of Vater Johann, and prayed that he might come to no harm as a result of helping them. Then her thoughts turned to Robin. She had no fear that Herr Borkel would not do all he could to get the little girl into safety. Four years before, Jem Russell had taken the Borkels' treasured only child up to the free ward at the Sanatorium for treatment, and had returned her to them cured. For that reason, neither Herr Borkel nor his wife would hesitate to do all they could for the Sonnalpe people. Robin, at least, was safe. For the others, she must trust in God that they would reach the haven of the Sonnalpe. But it was certain that the girls, at least, must leave Tyrol at once—she must go herself, too, most likely, though she was not sure if the crowd had grasped the fact that she was with them. But Jo, Robin, and Cornelia were all in grave danger. And the trouble might react on the Sonnalpe authorities. Then she put that worry aside, and slipped an arm round Daisy, who was already tired out and beginning to whimper.

'Cheer up, Daisy! It can't be so much further, and then we'll be safe. Tomorrow, you go to Guernsey with Mummy and the others, and there'll be no more of this.'

'Bill—*Robin*?' said Jo desperately.

'I left her to the Borkels. Don't worry, Jo. They'll get her up to Die Rosen if it's humanly possible. And she certainly isn't fit for this particular promenade. I wonder where on earth we shall come out?'

Up, and up, and up! The way seemed never-ending. They spoke but little. They were too tired, and too much overcome by memories of all they had endured. But at length the long weary way came to an end. First a grey light shone straight before them. Then it grew and grew, till at at once they found themselves struggling through an entanglement of briars, and they were out in the sweet, fresh air once more.

'Where are we?' demanded Jo, looking round. Suddenly, she uttered a cry of amazement. 'Why! Don't you see? We've come out by Robin's cave! Here's the entrance—and there's where I caught that little wretch of a Hermann.' Her quick mind leapt to a conclusion. 'Of course! The passage was built during the times when the priests had often to flee from Protestant persecution. They took refuge in that cave, and that cairn of stones is the altar they built so that they could say Mass while they were in hiding! No wonder it was such a job to get here! Well, we'd better get home as fast as we can now.'

She turned to Miss Wilson as she spoke, and her jaw fell, and the colour drained from her cheeks. Miss Wilson caught her, for she was really afraid the girl was going to faint.

'Sit down, Jo!' she commanded sharply.

But Jo resisted all her efforts at seating her. 'Miss Wilson! Your *hair*!' she gasped.

'My hair?' Miss Wilson lifted a strand of the curly mop still flowing about her, and now the other girls were all staring at her with the same expression of stupefaction. As she saw her hair, she ceased to wonder. It was snow-white!

CHAPTER X

FLIGHT!

F LIGHT was the immediate result of the wild
adventure. Flight for Joey and Miss Wilson, Hilary,
Jeanne, Maria, Lorenz, Evadne, and Cornelia. Daisy
was so little that they hoped she had not been noticed
and might go safely with her mother. And Robin, brought
up to Die Rosen at midnight by a fearful Herr Borkel,
was thought to be fairly safe as well, although, as Jem
said, it might be better for her if she went too. Jack
Maynard was included in the arrangements, for the girls
could scarcely wander over Europe unprotected. And
they insisted that Gottfried Mensch must join them. So
far he had been left alone; but it was certain that this
could not last. He must get away, and join his wife and
parents in Genoa.

Once she had got over the shock of learning that she
had literally turned white over the affair, Miss Wilson became her usual crisp, incisive self. They must not go
down to the Sonnalpe. Doubtless the place was already
watched. But the herdsmen were up on a shelf above it,
and Joey was known and beloved by them all. She must
take Daisy, hand her over to one of them, and ask him
to take the small girl home. These wild mountain-men
were little likely to be infected with the Nazi taint as yet,
and could be trusted. Daisy was to tell the story, and
say where they were. The rest must be left to the Sonnalpe people.

It was impressed on tired Daisy that she was to say
nothing to anyone outside. Let it be assumed that she had
gone for a walk, wandered away, and lost herself. Meanwhile, the party would seek refuge in the cave.

Thither came Jem, late at night, carrying a dozen useful
things in the big pockets of his shooting jacket. Coffee

and sandwiches were very grateful to the poor girls who were drowsing exhaustedly beside the little altar, while Miss Wilson kept watch at the entrance to the cave. Daisy had told how 'Bill's' hair had gone white, so the doctor was prepared for it, but he got a shock, all the same, when he saw her with a white crown where, in the morning, it had been rich chestnut brown.

'Poor Nell! What an experience!' he said as he followed her along the narrow passage. 'Never mind. The poudré effect is quite becoming'

'Oh, you!' Miss Wilson gave a queer laugh. 'As if it mattered! Here we are.—Come along, girls! Wake up! Here's Dr Jem and supper!'

The girls fell like hungry wolves on the food he had brought, and soon demolished it. Then they sat back, and the real business began.

'What about Robin?' demanded Jo, almost before she had taken her first bite. 'Is she safe, Jem?'

'Fast asleep in her own bed when I came out,' he replied. 'Herr Borkel brought her up about two hours ago.'

'What about poor Herr Goldmann? Did he escape all right?'

'No,' said Jem shortly.

'No? But I thought the Borkels took him through?'

'The crowd went to his place after. Herr Goldmann is dead, and his wife is dying. They shot Vater Johann too, but he is still living. He saved the Blessed Sacrament, so he is quite happy.'

There was a moment's silence. Then Jo spoke. 'Jem, are they after us? Have you had any of the police up?'

'Naturally. I was very anxious until Daisy arrived with Otto, weeping copiously. Mercifully no one had recognised her, and any questioners had accepted the story that she had lost herself on the mountainside and been found by Otto. She will be off tomorrow with Margot and the other kids. Rob and Herr Borkel had rather a bad time reaching us unseen. However, they managed it. But I daren't take you people back with me. They are waiting for you at the Sonnalpe. You've got to get away from here. Gottfried and Jack will try to slip away. I want Gottfried out of this; and it will be as well if Jack goes too. But this afternoon's exploit has finished the School. Madge and Miss Annersley have had warning that it must close down at once. The Nazis will take over the building.'

'Are they taking over the San?' asked Cornelia.

'Probably. I have no official news about that. But now we must see what we can do for you folk. You can't stay here. If it weren't such an awful night, they'd probably have had search-parties out after you, but there's a heavy mist. The clouds are right down, so you're safe for the next few hours. The question is, what shall we do with you?'

'Could we get into Switzerland?' suggested Jo hopefully.

He shook his head. 'None of your passports are right. It couldn't be done. I thought of it, but Gottfried says you must have your papers in order. And the same applies to Italy, of course.'

'Jem! What about Belsornia?' Joe was looking hopefully at him.

'Belsornia? I hadn't thought of that. If only we could get word to the King, it could be done. Otherwise, I'm afraid the passport difficulty would be the same as elsewhere.'

'If we could manage to hide somewhere for the next day or two, could you get word to him, do you think?'

Jem considered. 'Where do you propose to hide?'

'In the Zillerthal. They aren't likely to look for us there. I know of a place—Frieda showed it to me, when we spent the summer there last year—that would be safe if we could only get there.'

'If you got there, how would you manage for food?'

'If we stay here, we'll be no better off so far as food goes,' urged Joey. 'You've managed to feed us now; but you won't have much chance of doing it a second time. Look here, Jem, go back, and tell Jack and Gottfried to get away at once if they can, and meet us at Umfert. Tell them to bring all the concentrated foodstuff they can, and some dry clothes too; also, what cash they can tuck in. Then we'll make tracks for the Vierfesthütte. The place is somewhere near there. One of us will come to the Hütte every day at dusk, and they can meet us there. I don't know how they'll get us out, but they'll manage it somehow if I know the King and Veta.' She spoke of the young Crown Princess of Belsornia, who had once spent two happy terms as boarder at the Chalet School. Princess Elizaveta was now eighteen, and a very important person in her little world, but she still retained a wholehearted friendship for Jo, who had, in the days when both were wild Middles, saved her from the plots of her father's cousin and heir, a partial madman, who had tried to kidnap her. Belsornians are a warm-hearted race, and they were devoted to Jo, who had certainly risked her life in saving their princess. Jem knew that once the girls were safe in Belsornia, it was only a matter of time before they reached England. Jo's idea had been a good one. The only difficulty would be how to get word to the King.

'I've brought you some tins of concentrated beef and chicken juice,' he said, rising and hauling them from his pockets. 'Also this travelling etna and a bottle of methylated spirit. Here's a billy-can to boil water in, and three boxes of matches. I must get back in case I am asked for. Now, as soon as I've gone, you clear up here, and get off. I'll tell Jack and Gottfried to meet you at Umfert. Then you must manage for yourselves. Here's a couples of torches, and two spare batteries. Don't use them if you can help it. And for mercy's sake be careful how you get down the mountain. Goodbye, Miss Wilson.— Goodbye, girls.—Joey-baba, take care of yourself.' He held Jo close for a moment, murmuring something in her ear. Then he released her, and departed. They heard his footsteps dying away down the passage, and they were alone again. Jo, with a startled expression on her face, turned to helping to clear up, for they must leave no traces of their presence here. Every crumb had to be hidden. The paper which had wrapped the sandwiches was folded, and tucked into blazer-pockets. Silver paper from chocolate was retrieved. Finally, when everything was done, the tins of meat juices, the stove and the bottle of methylated spirit were shared out, and with the feeling that they were in for the biggest adventure of their careers, they passed down the dark passage, and out into a world heavily veiled in fog.

Miss Wilson led the way. Feeling carefully with a long stick she had picked up under the pines, she went steadily down, now and then consulting her little pocket compass by means of one of the torches. It was nearly three o'clock in the morning, and it would soon be light, for this was June. The thick mist, however, gave no indication of daylight, and everywhere was quiet.

They reached the bottom just as a village clock near by chimed the hour of eight. The mist was still thick over everything, and they could scarcely see two yards before them. The result of this was that Cornelia, walking carelessly, set her foot on a thick bulk, and fell flat, while a great pig rising to its feet tore off, screaming its woes to the world.

In great alarm, the others pulled Corney up again, and bolted for some trees near at hand, where they took cover and waited. But on such a day no one bothered much about the squealing of a pig, and no one came to investigate. So the refugees went on, for this was not Umfert, which Joey reckoned to be at least an hour ahead.

'Once we get there, we can hide easily,' she said. 'Then we'll have some beef-tea or chicken-broth, and that will warm us.'

Miss Wilson looked anxiously at them. While in the cave, they had done their best to tidy themselves. But all had wet shoes and stockings, thanks to the mist, and they were white-faced and heavy-eyed from the sleepless night. However, they must just go on. Once they had reached their hiding-place, they could have all the rest they wanted—probably too much; for it was unlikely that any message could be got to Belsornia under three or four days; and then there would be the difficulty of getting them away.

It was at this point that Jo turned back, looking rather

red. 'Bill,' she said apprehensively, 'I rather think I've lost us.'

'You've what? Do talk English, Joey!'

'I've lost us. We ought to be getting to Umfert by this time, and we seem to be miles away. I've just seen a board over there which says Wehlten, and I know that's a good hour away to the north. We'll have to turn to the right. I do hope Jack and Gottfried aren't waiting about for us. It'll be even worse for thèm than for us.'

Miss Wilson said nothing. It was no use. But she produced her compass again, and watched it closely for the next hour. By that time they were all dead tired, and Jeanne complained of a blister on her heel. But they were within sound of Umfert, for Jo recognised the chimes of the village clock, which were peculiarly deep in tone. At the same moment, the sound of heavy boots on the road sent them, in great alarm, into the deep ditch which ran down its side.

It was a tall man who came along, clad in peasant's clothes, and yodelling as he went. At sight of him, Joey scrambled out of the ditch, exclaiming, 'Gottfried!'

'Here you are, then,' he said casually.

'Where's Jack?' demanded Jo.

'I do not know. He left two hours before I did with Robin, and——'

'With Robin? Why? Jeem thought she'd be all right? What's happened?'

'Steady, Jo,' said Gottfried, for she looked rather as though she might fly at him and shake the information out of him. 'It's all right. At least, it isn't; but Rob is safely away. After Jem had left, two men from the police came, demanding her. However, Madge put them off somehow, and then sent Jack for me. We decided that she must be got away at once; so he left at four, when Jem came back to tell us what you were going to do. I left at six, and they were to meet me here. It is all right, for the mist is even heavier at the Sonnalpe than here, and there is no possibility of anyone making any search. I got here first because I know the ways, I expect. Now, we must hide and wait. I have fresh clothes for all of you in my pack which I left in yonder barn. Come along, all of you, and you shall be dry and comfortable once more.'

He led the way to a big barn where, hidden at the back of the wheat-stack, was a huge pack, such as pedlars use in Tyrol, and in it were warm, dry clothes for them all—Tyrolean clothes, as Jo instantly saw. Gottfried retired to a corner, and they hastened to change. Then they folded up their own attire, and, feeling very much better came out.

'Plait your hair, Miss Wilson,' he told that lady, eyeing the snowy locks with interest. 'Take it straight back, and plait it, and coil it as the country women do. Joey also.— And you two as well,' he added to Cornelia and Evadne, who both possessed mops reaching beyond their shoulders. Jeanne had already fastened her hair, for Madge had tucked in three packets of hairpins. Hilary's hair was bobbed, but Gottfried tied a handkerchief over it, hiding the short ends. When they were done at length, they looked, so far as a casual glance was concerned, like a peasant woman and her family. But Hilary would never really look anything else but English. And Jo's distinction of face and figure was not easy to disguise. Worst of all, the hands of all of them were a distinct 'give away.' Gottfried advised them to make them dirty, and trusted to luck that no one would examine them closely enough to note that such nails and fingers were not those of peasant girls.

'One of us ought to have been a boy,' said Cornelia. 'You could have hacked Hilary's bob and put her into boy's things. It would have been even better than making all of us girls.'

But Gottfried thought that the less disguise there had to be the better. As it was, the elder girls moved awkwardly in their unaccustomed long skirts. Trousers would have been too much for Hilary, he felt sure. He shook his head at Cornelia, and went out to see if he could see anything of Jack Maynard and the Robin, for, secretly, he was growing very worried at their non-appearance.

He strolled down the road, yodelling softly to himself, apparently as carefree a young peasant as anyone could meet, and he was rewarded, for, coming down the road, were the two people he was seeking. Jack Maynard also wore a peasant's dress, with braces, leather breeches, little hat with cock's feather at the back, and full-sleeved shirt. The Robin wore the dress of a little Tyrolean girl, with a large shawl over her head, for her pretty curls were, like Hilary's, bobbed.

Gottfried broke into a rapid stride when he saw them, for it needed no keen sight to tell him that something had gone badly wrong.

'What's up, man?' he demanded when he was close to them.

'Rob and I have been spotted. I'm sure of it. We must get off as fast as we can. We can't draw your people into this, you know. And we must get the girls out of the place as soon as possible. Tell you all about it later. At present, let's be off!'

Gottfried said no more. Swinging Robin up in his arms —a liberty which, secretly, her fourteen-year-old dignity resented—he strode on to the barn, Jack at his side, and they hastily summoned Miss Wilson and the girls, bidding them come at once.

'Lucky we cleared up everything,' said Joey, her black eyes gleaming brilliantly in her pale face as she felt Jack's clasp on her arm. 'Rob, my darling, come here. Where do we go, Gottfried?'

'Down this ditch,' said Gottfried. 'Quick, now! Then through that gap in the hedge, and along the hedge to the woods. Hasten!'

They hurried along and at length gained the woods, where Gottfried took them down little bypaths, warning them to be careful how they trod. They went on and on, getting deeper and deeper into the wood, until Joey wondered how on earth Gottfried was able to find his way. But he led straight ahead, and by noon they were many miles from the farm. They sat down for a hurried meal, and then Jack told his story.

All had gone well until he had reached the plain, when, just an hour before they met Gottfried, two men, plainly Gestapo agents, had stopped to ask them the way somewhere. Jack had shaken his head as if he did not understand. His German was fluent enough; but he knew no patois, and he judged it best to say nothing. The man had then turned to Robin. But he had been one of those who had first visited the Sonnalpe, and had seen her, and her angelic loveliness was not to be forgotten. He uttered an exclamation which told Jack that they were recognised. There was only one thing to do. Grabbing the pair of them by their necks, he had knocked their heads together with such good will that they ceased to take interest in anyone or anything for at least another five minutes; and during that five minutes, with Robin tossed over his shoulder, the young doctor had made his escape. But he knew that if they were met again, they would be recognised, and then, indeed, heavy would be the retribution that would befall them.

Jo gave a cry, and flung an arm round him. 'Oh, Jack! Oh, my dear!'

'No time for that, Joey,' said Gottfried quietly. 'We must get on. But we dare not go to the Zillerthal now. We must risk it, and make for Switzerland.'

CHAPTER XI

ESCAPE!

THERE was nothing else for it. If they remained in this district they were almost certain to be caught, and the Zillerthal was too near. But how they were to get a party of girls, including a delicate child like Robin, into Switzerland, which lay many long and weary leagues to the west, was a problem the two young men found difficult to tackle. The only thing to do was to go on, and trust to Gottfried's intimate knowledge of the district to help them. At least, it was still misty, even here in the woods. They found later that almost all Tyrol had suffered from that heavy fog.

Gottfried got up. 'We must go,' he said abruptly. 'We will rest again soon, though.'

Joey slipped her hand through her fiancé's free arm, clinging to him as if she dreaded being parted from him. He looked down into her pale face and smiled.

'Oh, Jack!' she said under her breath: 'They mustn't get you—they *mustn't* get you!'

'Heart up, Joey darling! God willing, we shall escape, though it's a long road before us. Madge sent you a message. She is praying for us all, night and day, and she knows we shall be safe. Hello! What's Gottfried after now?' For Gottfried had set Lorenz on the ground, and flung himself down flat.

'He thinks he hears something,' said Jo fearfully.

Gottfried was up again, however, and was smiling. 'Only an old ass,' he said. 'But for a moment—I feared——' he left his sentence unfinished.

It was growing dusk when at length they paused for a real rest. Gottfried had given them ten-minute halts during the long walk, but now he led them into a little natural cave made of furze bushes, and bade them sleep after they had had something to eat. He and Jack vanished with the etna and the pan, and a couple of tins, and presently they reappeared with a panful of strong, hot soup which was nectar to the poor, weary girls. Miss Wilson had broken a small bone in her foot some years before, and though it had healed well, it ached when she strained it, and now she was wondering how she could possibly hobble on. However, Gottfried promised them all four hours of rest, and they could face their problems better after sleep.

When the time was up, Gottfried woke automatically, and prepared another meal. Then he woke the rest, though it went to his heart to see how white and weary they all looked. Most of them were only children, however plucky they might be. The young Austrian ground his teeth together as he thought how, in his proud, free land, things had come to such a pass that schoolgirls must be fleeing before the government.

83

He said nothing of his thoughts, but Joey, with her queer gift of insight, guessed at them, and as he gave her her cup of soup, she put her hand on his for a moment. 'Gottfried! It isn't *you*; it's the Nazis. We don't blame you; we don't even blame the German people for all this.'

The stern lines on his face relaxed. 'Thank you, Joey. But to those of us who love our country and are proud of her record of liberty, it is a terrible thought that no one can now be free in the land where Andreas Hofer gave his all for freedom.'

Then he went on to give Miss Wilson her soup. 'What is wrong, Miss Wilson? You are in pain; I can see it in your face. Are you ill?'

'Bill' shook her head. 'Only my foot—you remember that old break? It's aching rather badly. That's all.'

Gottfried finished his present duty. Then he called Jack Maynard, and together they examined the foot. It was swollen, and obviously very painful, but there was little they could do. It needed rest, and rest was the one thing they could not give it. But Gottfried pulled off the kerchief round his neck and strapped it up as tightly as he could, and Miss Wilson said she could manage.

For five days they walked, often hungry, almost always aching. The two youngest girls were carried whenever it was possible, but Jack and Gottfried were tiring more quickly now, for food was scant, and they had gone on for so long. Over and over again they had to slip through holes and into ditches to avoid being seen. On one occasion, when Jo and Jack and Robin had got left behind and they had no chance to hide anywhere, they heard a band of mounted riders coming after them. Jo breathed a prayer for help, and when the men drew abreast with them, called out to them in Romany, of which she knew a phrase or two, holding out her hand for an alms in true Romany fashion. She had to dodge a cut from a whip, and was freely cursed, but the men rode past, never dreaming that the fugitives they were after had spoken with them.

The others of the little party had been able to hide, and were horrified when they heard of the narrow escape.

But Jo grinned one of her old grins for the first time since they had been forced to flee.

'Not much to worry about,' she said cheerfully. 'Did you ever see such hooligans as we look? I offered to tell their fortunes in Romany, and got nicely sworn at for my pains. But I'll bet they'd no idea it was *me*, so to speak.'

'I would like to go to bed,' said Robin drowsily. 'I *am* so tired!'

They looked at her in alarm. She was not yet very far from the day when her health had been a constant worry, and there was no doubt that this terrible journey had tried her highly. Even Evadne and Cornelia, strong, healthy girls as they were, had had enough. As for Jeanne, frailer than the others, she looked so ill as she lay back against Hilary's arm flung protectingly round her that Jack Maynard glanced at Gottfried and raised his brows.

'Not a great deal further now,' said the latter with a cheerfulness he did not really feel. 'We've come to the mountains again, and if we can only get through by a secret road I know, we shall be safe. I am taking you all to an aunt of mine. Joey, you have heard Frieda speak of Tante Anna? She lives just across the frontier. She will befriend us, I know. We will all go to her.'

'It's to be hoped she has a large house, then,' said Joey with a giggle. She was so tired that she was inclined to be hysterical. 'Otherwise, I don't see where she's going to put us all.'

Jack shook her. 'Stop that, Jo! Even if you are tired, you needn't make a fool of yourself! We're not there yet. Just wait till you're safe before you begin any hysterical nonsense!'

His intentional roughness roused Jo to self-control, and she sat up rather indignantly. 'Don't be so brutal, Jack. I'm all right.'

'Then see you *keep* all right,' he told her severely. 'We've enough on our hands without you being stupid! — Gottfried, isn't time up? Then we'd better get on. I'd like to be on that secret road of yours as soon as possible. I'd feel a long way safer then.'

Gottfried took the hint. 'Up you get!' he said. 'With luck, we'll soon be on the last lap of our journey.'

They set off on what they hoped would be the last dangerous part of their flight. By evening they were among the mountains, and toiling up a narrow track shielded on both sides by great bushes and tall pines. It was cooler here, and that was a relief, for since the first day the sun had poured down on them with a cruel heat which had added to the trials of the journey. At length they reached the pass for which Gottfried was making. It was difficult, and very rarely used on that account. Nor did he intend to use it all the time. They *might* meet travellers, and it was as well to keep from view as much as possible. Besides which, if they were to have no trouble over papers and passports, they must go by what was known as 'the smugglers' way.' It added considerably to the length and difficulty of the journey, but it also added to their safety, and that mattered most just now.

Of the last part of the journey, once they were in the pass, not one of them ever cared to think, once it was all over. It seemed to be made up of a series of climbs over stones—now up, now down. At one time, they had to walk knee-deep through a rushing mountain stream, where the strong current nearly took them off their feet, and the icy water chilled them through and through. Then out again, and over the stony way once more, greatly to their astonishment, with easier feet. Gottfried smiled when they exclaimed, and told them that the cold water cure was one of the best for foot soreness.

They ate their scanty midday meal in a cleft high up among the rocks, and saw a small body of German police pass along the road to the Swiss frontier. Luckily, they were out of sight, but until the men had vanished down the road, they dared scarcely draw breath.

'No fear need trouble you,' said Gottfried, when at length all was safe again. 'We go up now, and here there is a spur which hides us from them. Nor can they see us as we go across the spur, for our path is hollowed out, and a low wall of rock protects us from their sight. So it is all safe. We will rest just a little longer, and then we must go, for I do not wish to be caught in the pathway by nightfall. It will be cold up there then.—Miss Wilson, we are going to bind up your foot again, and I trust you can go until we reach our resting-place for the night, for the path is narrow, with room for only one at a time. But we will do our best to make you comfortable.'

As he spoke, he took off his leather belt, produced his knife, and cut a piece of leather which he proceeded to trim till it fitted into Miss Wilson's instep. This was bound tightly into place with Jack Maynard's scarf, and Bill declared that she could manage quite well now. But, despite her bravery, it was all she could do to reach the cave where Gottfried decreed they should spend the night-hours. Then she sank down in a semi-unconscious state from which they roused her with difficulty. However, Gottfried had got coffee earlier in the day from a kindly housewife. It is true that it was mainly chicory and bitter, but it did her good, and she even managed to eat some of the very dry roll he crumbled into the coffee. But when the meal was over, she lay back almost grey with pain, and the two doctors saw that she was at the end of her tether. However they managed it, they must carry her on the morrow.

Strangely enough, the coming back to the mountains had revived the Robin. A faint colour tinged her cheeks, and her eyes were brighter. She ate her share of the food with appetite, and when it was done, curled up in Joey's arms, and fell fast asleep. Jo was more of a problem. Sensitive and finely strung, never of robust constitution, she had suffered severely by the strain, and Gottfried was inclined to fear the effects of the reaction, once she was in safety. Miss Wilson was another problem, for it seemed as if her foot might be permanently weakened by the heavy strain put on it.

'I am less anxious about Robin,' murmured Gottfried, as he sat with his friend, smoking a luxurious cigarette, while the girls slept. 'She is reviving up here. But I do not like Miss Wilson's foot.'

'Nor do I,' said Jack seriously. 'I'm afraid—it may mean permanent lameness. And I'm very much afraid for Joey. Upon my word, Gottfried, I've a very good mind to give her something to make her sleep for two or three days when we get to your aunt's.'

Gottfried shook his head. 'I do not think it would do. Jo is a bad subject for drugs. However, we will see.'

It was late when the two doctors slept, but they woke early. There was promise of a fine day, and, as they looked round at the sleeping girls, they felt that the night's quiet rest, up there near the mountain snows, had done much for them. Robin looked almost herself; so did Lorenz. Jeanne's little face was faintly pink; and Hilary and the two Americans were fresh and rosy. The grey look had left Miss Wilson's face, and the lines of pain were smoothed out. Even Jo had lost the bruises under her eyes. The two men lit the etna and made chocolate with stick chocolate and water from the glacier stream rushing along a little further on. It was all they had for breakfast but a couple of very stale rolls which were broken up into the chocolate. However, Gottfried expected they would be with his aunt shortly after midday, and then they would get a proper meal. They roused the girls and Miss Wilson.

'Heigh-ho!' yawned Jo. 'I was having such a lovely dream, all about last summer. Why did you wake me?'

'Come to breakfast,' said Jack Maynard with a grin. 'It's all ready—only waiting to be—er—taken.'

'I'm glad you didn't say "eaten"!' ejaculated Jo as she surveyed her share. 'Is that all? I could eat an elephant if I had one handy.'

'Don't be greedy,' said Cornelia reprovingly. 'Though I must say breakfast is a bit scarce,' she added, looking at her cupful.

They were so near safety that they were able to relax a little, and that last meal as fugitives was eaten with laughter and jesting such as they had not indulged in for six long days now. When it was over, Miss Wilson's foot was bathed and bound up again. Then Gottfried slung her round his shoulders in a 'fireman's lift,' and, with a long stick made from a pine-tree bough for alpenstock, he led the way, followed by Hilary and Lorenz, Evadne and Robin, Cornelia and Jeanne, and Joey and Jack bringing up the rear.

The way was not dangerous or difficult, but it was sufficiently toilsome, and they had one very nasty moment when the figure of a Swiss gendarme showed up on the horizon for a moment. Swiss gendarmes at the frontier are armed, and they have no scruples about shooting at smugglers, who, thereabouts, are a hardy, daring set of fellows, and as ready to shoot at the gendarmes. Luckily, something distracted his attention, and in the five minutes his head was turned, they had dashed across the frontier into Switzerland. They were safe at last!

CHAPTER XII

THE CHALET SCHOOL REVIVES

'AUNTIE JO!'

Jo—no longer Jo Bettany, but for the past ten months Jo Maynard—lifted her head from the sheaf of long galley proofs over which she had been frowning and biting her pencil, and smiled at her nephews and nieces who were clustered round the open French window.

'Hello, chickabids! Mummy tired of you all? Come along in and sit down, and we'll see what there is to eat in the place.'

'Gâche!' suggested Peggy Bettany with an angelic smile.

'Gâche, if I can find it. Leave those proofs alone, Rix! If you muddle them up, I'll have just twice the work to do, and then, my lad, no gâche for you!'

Rix, who had been fingering the proofs, jumped back from the table in haste. He always wanted to play with those fascinating long strips of print. But gâche was even better than galley proofs.

Meanwhile, Joey had gone to a cupboard they all knew, and was producing a fresh gâche, that Guernsey cut-and-come-again cake which is one of the best things in the world for satisfying an appetite sharpened by Guernsey fresh air. She got a knife and sent Peggy to the kitchen to get milk.

'Mummy's sent a message, Auntie Joe,' said David, now a sturdy boy of just seven. '*An*' two letters. Peg's got them.'

'A message? Why on earth didn't you give it to me sooner? What is it?'

'Only to come to tea this afternoon,' said Primula Mary, still tiny, and crowned with a straight shock of primrose-coloured hair. Primula Mary and her sister Daisy were motherless now, Margot Venables having slipped away from them six months before. She had never really recovered from the grief or her boys' deaths, and all she had undergone in Austria. The wild anxiety of those last weeks in Tyrol had finished a system already undermined, and she had faded tranquilly out of life, knowing that her two little girls would be safe with her brother and his wife. Primula was too young to realise her loss, but twelve-year-old Daisy had grieved for her, and only lately had she recovered her lost merriment.

She now backed up her small sister's statement. 'Auntie Madge had letters this morning, Auntie Jo. One was from America, 'cos she gave me the stamp for my c'llection. She took them to Uncle Jem, and then she said we were to come and tell you to come to tea this afternoon.'

'All right. Are those the letters Peg's got for me?' asked Jo cheerfully, as she cut generous hunks of gâche. 'Hello, Peg! Where are those letters? Hand them over. I want to see Auntie Marie's.'

Peggy felt in her sailor blouse, and produced two letters which she handed over, and while the small folk feasted, their aunt sat down in her chair, after putting the proofs into a basket, and began to read.

The first was from her old chum, Marie von und zu Wertheimer.

90

'Dearest Madame,' Marie had written, 'This is to let you know that we are tired of America, lovely though our visit has been. We can't go home, now that the Nazis have requisitioned the Castle. Besides, Eugen was ordered home by them weeks ago, and he took no notice of it. If he sets foot in Tyrol so long as they are there, it will mean bad trouble for him. At the same time, we don't intend to become Americans, so we have decided to pay a visit to your happy island. Can you get a house for us? It need not be very large. I have been very independent since I have been over here. So if you can find one which has three sitting-rooms and six bedrooms, I think we can manage.

'Eugen and I still have little Josefa with us; and Wolferl sleeps in Eugen's dressing-room. Then Wanda and her pair will come. Poor Wanda! She tries to be brave; but there has been no news from Friedel for nearly nine months now. We can only hope that he is dead. One hears such dreadful stories about concentration camps. At least, she has the children to comfort her. They would want only a bedroom, for Maria Ileana sleeps with Wanda, and Keferl can go in with our Wolferl. Besides these, we want two rooms for the maids, and one to turn into a nursery. Even Keferl is hardly old enough for school yet; and, of course, the other three are only babies. If we *could* have a garden, it would be nice, for they are all very out-of-doors little people, and we would like them to continue to be so. Write soon, please, and let us know what you can do.—Love to everyone, MARIE.'

Jo folded up the letter with a laugh, and turned to the other, which was from Miss Stewart, who, since the closing down of the School and the dispersal of its inmates, had been putting in her time paying visits among her relations. They had not been able to restart the School at once, for, two months after Joey's wedding, a small sister had come for David and Sybil. Then the entire party of small folk had elected to go in for chicken-pox, and by the time that was over, the winter had come, and Mrs Russell thought it wiser to wait till the spring.

Now, however, Miss Stewart, wearying of perpetual holiday, had written, demanding to know when they were to begin again.

'It was quite fun jaunting about at first,' she wrote. 'I saw everyone I hadn't really seen for years. But now I'm sick of doing nothing. So is Nell Wilson, with whom I am staying. She has a ducky little cottage here, and it's great fun, but, like myself, she wants to get back into harness again. So what about it?

'*Do* think it over, and think it over favourably. Can't Joey help; or has she gone all domesticated and house-keepery? I'm not to be married for another year, as Jock has just got a new appointment in Singapore, and wants to go out first to see what the climate and so on is like. I had a big hand in the Tyrolean Chalet School. I'd like to have a finger in the pie when you start the new one. So stir your stumps, my child, and get going. Your new daughter can't be an awful bother now, and you can spare time to begin us, I'm sure. Do; please do!

'My salaams to everyone, including Baby Josette.
                                        CON STEWART.'

Joey chuckled aloud as she folded up this letter, and Daisy at once cocked her head. 'What is the joke, Auntie Jo?'

'You'll hear later, I don't doubt,' said Jo. 'Well, what are you folk going to do with yourselves today?'

'Rosalie and Grizel are taking us to Pleinmont for a picnic,' said David blandly.

His aunt caught him up at once. '*Aunt* Rosalie and *Aunt* Grizel, young man, if you please. Anyone else coming?'

'Gillian and Joyce Linton,' said Daisy. 'Auntie asked them over the 'phone, and they said they would. They're bringing a new friend they've met in Peterport. She has lots of children—five, I think—to look after, and she's going to bring some of them.'

'What's happening to the ones she's not bringing?'

'They'll stay at home with their mummy.'

'Oh, I see. She isn't their mummy, then? What is her name, d'you know, or didn't Gill and Joyce tell you?'

'It's Miss La Touche. She's governess to them, and some others as well, but they're all at home with colds, so they can't come. But Joyce said that Julie and John would come, and *perhaps* Betsy.'

'How old are they?' asked Jo.

'Julie is about David's age, and John is a little younger, I think. Betsy is three or four, but I'm not sure.'

'No one of your age, then. I wish there had been.' Jo looked serious. Since they had settled in Guernsey, the children had had lessons at home from herself, with Rosalie Dene and Grizel Cochrane to help. They had made no new friends, and she often thought that it would be better for Daisy if she had friends of her own age.

'Joyce says that Miss La Touche told her that Nancy Chester—she's one of the ones with cold—has a sister just my age,' explained the young lady. 'She'll come another time, perhaps. Auntie Jo, don't you think I could go to school with her? She goes to one in Peterport. It would be—rather nice, I think.'

Joey shook her head. 'Too far for you, my lamb. We're right at the other end of the Island, and you would be dreadfully tired with the journey every day. Now, you people, finish your gâche and milk, and trot off and say I'm coming to Bonne Maison this afternoon. But I can't play with you. I must get these proofs done.' And she cast a distasteful glance at the proofs.

The small fry finished their elevenses and departed. Joey sat down, and worked with such a will that one o'clock saw her packing up the hated proofs, ready to post on her way to Bonne Maison, the house the Russells had finally settled in, at Torteval. The Maynards themselves were in a small villa not far from St Pierre du Bois, about an hour's walk away. It was a small house, but suited them for the present, though Joey was already talking of leaving and going nearer her sister when she could find something suitable.

After lunch, which she had alone, since Jack was with

Jem, lunching with Dr Chester, the leading medico of the Island, she got out her little Singer car, and drove through the narrow, flowery lanes across the Island to Bonne Maison, an old farmhouse which Madge had turned into a charming home for her family. They had been able to bring most of their possessions from Tyrol, though some had had to be left behind, and the children enjoyed the novelty of open fires, carpeted floors, and beds without plumeaux, which are never necessary in the warm climate of Guernsey.

At the door, Madge Russell came to meet her young sister, her last baby in her arms. The terrible experiences they had all gone through had brought silver threads to her hair, but her eyes were as steadfast, her smile as sweet as ever.

Jo waved her hand gaily. 'Hello, Madge! I've brought the letters with me. What fun to start the School again! But where will you put it? It can't be here—there isn't room.' She had left the car by this time, and was enveloping her sister and goddaughter in a bear's hug that drew a yell of protest from the latter, and made Madge remark, 'Don't be so violent, Joey! You're frightening Josette.'

'Give her to me, Madge. Come to Godmamma, pet!' And Joey rocked the small creature lovingly as she followed her sister into the pretty drawing-room which had once been the farm kitchen. 'What about the School?' she asked.

'Well, I think we might try now,' said Madge cautiously. 'Jem heard yesterday of an old house that might be made habitable. It's not far from Jerbourg, where they intend to have the Sanatorium. Of course, it'll have to be a small beginning, as Con Stewart suggests. We haven't the money for all our wonderful apparatus, and so on. But I'm content to begin that way.'

'Let's see. How about Staff? We shall have Con Stewart, and Hilda Annersley, and Nell Wilson. Then Simone will come for maths, and Grizel will be resident music as before, I suppose. Shall you ask Ivy Norman to come for Kindergarten? Is she free?'

'No; she's got a very good post in a big school near London, and I couldn't ask her to throw it up for us. But May Phipps wasn't happy where she was, so I think I'll write and suggest she comes to us.'

'And Vater Bär for those people who are good enough, I suppose, and Plato for singing,' supplemented Jo. 'Oh, well, we can manage all right for Staff. Will Jeanne Lachenais come back for languages? I know she said she wanted to.'

'I haven't had time to write yet. But I expect it will be all right.'

'What is the name of the house, by the way? Do I know it?'

'You've passed it many a time. It's Sarres, that big old place.'

'What? The Moated Grange! My dear, it's a wreck! However can you put it in order? 'Tisn't as if money was awfully plentiful at present, you know. We've lost a good deal over the Sonnalpe.'

'No; but Jem says it's not so bad inside as outside. The structure is in pretty good repair, and we must just do it as cheaply as we can. Mercifully, we managed to retain all our stock and text-books, though I was afraid at one time they were going to keep them. And we have all the wall-maps, and a good deal of the science apparatus. Of course, we'll have to get school furniture, and that's always expensive. But we must do the best we can.'

It was a fascinating subject of conversation, and the sisters continued it until long after the small fry had come in, tired and rosy from their picnic, and been whisked off to bed by Marie and Rosa, who had come with the Russells from Tyrol. Indeed, it wasn't till Jem and Jack appeared, demanding supper, that it ended. Then, as Madge moved about, helping to lay the table, while Joey cut bread, and the men carved ham and filled up glasses with lemonade, Dr Russell turned to his wife.

'Well, got it all settled?' he inquired.

'I think so,' said Madge smilingly.

CHAPTER XIII

JOEY MAKES A NEW FRIEND

IT was August the thirtieth, and the day before the new version of the Chalet School was due to open. Dr Chester's wife, now a firm friend of Mrs Russell's, had advised beginning then, and not waiting till the middle of September like most of the English schools.

'We often begin autumn storms then,' she explained. 'You don't want your pupils to start with violent attacks of seasickness, do you?'

So the thirty-first of August had been set for the first day of term, and then it had been a case of all hands on deck, for to get the old house at Sarres into proper order was a fairly heavy task. It was very large, with big rooms, and a good number of them, downstairs. The bedrooms were smaller, but there were two storeys of them, besides the attics, which would make ideal domestic staff quarters. The paintwork was painted a deep, soft green; broken and cracked panes of glass were renewed in the windows, which were hung with the curtains of plain net that had come from Tyrol; what school furniture they had been able to save had been placed in position; and, as they had been able to bring all the prints and pictures they had formerly had, the rooms did not look too bare. The floors were stained black, and polished to within an inch of their lives by Mrs Russell's Marie and Rosa, and Joey's Anna, and gay rugs laid here and there redeemed them from a too austere look.

'It might be worse,' said Jo critically, as, with Robin and Daisy hanging on either arm, she made a tour of the place. 'The dining-room is quite nice, and so is Hall. A bit small, if we grow as we did in Tyrol; but that's not so very likely. Goodness knows what may happen in the near future,' she added, referring to the prospect of war with Germany, which seemed to be coming rapidly nearer—though even Jo could not see how near it was.

'We had nearly two hundred and fifty the last year,' said Robin wistfully. 'To fall back to *fifty-two* is a drop!'

'Lots of schools would be thankful and overjoyed if they started with half that number, my lamb. Mrs Chester was telling me yesterday that she knew of two girls who began a school with only *two* pupils. And they stayed at two pupils for two years. After that, they began to grow, and now they have a waiting-list, they are so popular.'

'Oh, I hope we don't stick at fifty-two for two years!' gasped Robin, whose fourteen months in England had robbed her of the last of her foreign accent and expressions, and turned her into a thoroughly English schoolgirl. She was fifteen now, and, for the last year, the thick black curls had been allowed to grow till now they were just long enough to tie up with two big bows at either side of her head.

Daisy had sprouted up lately, and was all arms and legs. Her thick honey-coloured hair was plaited into two plaits, and, in her brown tunic, with shantung top, and flame-coloured tie, she looked very pretty. She had begun to chatter again in the old way, and though her mother would never be forgotten, she had grown reconciled to her loss.

Jo was, in some ways, the most changed of the trio. Her marriage had developed the womanliness in her, and she was no longer a rough-and-tumble schoolgirl. Now she glanced out of the window. 'Someone is coming up the path—why, it's Mrs Lucy, Julie's mother. What can she want?'

'I hope it isn't to say that she's changed her mind about sending Julie and John,' said Daisy anxiously. 'We do want *some* new ones to add to all the old ones who are coming back.'

The smiling maid who had gone to answer the door, now appeared to say that Mrs Lucy had called to see Mrs Maynard. Joey cast a fleeting glance at her reflection in the nearest mirror, and left Daisy and Robin while she departed to the drawing-room where the visitor awaited her.

She knew Julie and John Lucy by this time; also the Chester children and the Ozanne twin girls. She had met Mrs Chester and her lovely sister, Mrs Ozanne. But so far, though she had heard plenty about her, she had not made the acquaintance of Mrs Lucy. A new baby had arrived in June at Les Arbres, the Lucy's beautiful old house at the other side of Peterport, and Mrs. Lucy had been very ill for some weeks. Even when she was able to be up and about, she had been kept quiet. And Jo and Jack had spent most of August at his people's home in the New Forest. They had returned home only just in time to welcome Marie von und zu Wertheimer and her family, including her lovely elder sister Wanda, and Wanda's two children. Wanda was very quiet and sad, for nothing had been heard of her husband, Friedel von Glück, for nearly ten months.

Mrs Chester and Mrs Ozanne were both exquisitely lovely women, and for this reason Joey had made up her mind that their youngest sister must be superlatively beautiful. She got a shock, therefore, when, on entering the drawing-room, she saw the reality.

Janie Lucy was not beautiful. She was not even pretty. Young Mrs Maynard found it hard to realise that this puckish-looking individual was the sister of two such beautiful women.

Mrs. Lucy knew what Jo was thinking, of course, for there wasn't much that escaped her eyes. She had seen it happen before, and suddenly she grinned outright, whereat Jo turned a startled look on her and then blushed scarlet to the roots of her black hair.

'You don't know how to reconcile me with Elizabeth and Anne, Mrs Maynard,' said the visitor confidentially. 'I—I—' stammered Jo, the scarlet deepening to purple in her confusion.

Mrs Lucy chuckled. 'Oh, I've seen it before, my dear. It's hard luck on me, isn't it? Luckily, I married a handsome man, and most of the children take after him, so it might be worse.'

Jo collapsed. 'You—you—' It was no good. She could go no further. She gave up all attempts at self-control, and shouted with laughter. Mrs Lucy joined in, giggling infectiously like a schoolgirl instead of the mother of five. When at length they both sat up, wiping their eyes, they were friends for life, and they knew it.

'That's better,' said Mrs Lucy, putting away her handkerchief. 'Now we can stop being polite and society and *talk*!'

'Come on and see the School,' invited Joey hospitably.

'I'd love to. That's one reason why I came, you know. Also to say how sorry I am that I haven't been able to call on you sooner. I've heard reams about you from my sisters, of course. You poor dear! What a time you've had! However, it's over now, and you ought to be able to get a book out of it anyhow, so that's some consolation.'

'I'm getting one this minute,' returned Jo, ushering her guest into the Kindergarten-room. 'This is where your small boy will be.'

'What a gorgeous place! I say! Have I got to call you "Mrs Maynard"? Or may we be Joey and Janie to each other?'

'Rather! It still makes me feel rather a fool when people call me "Mrs." It doesn't seem *me*, somehow.'

Janie Lucy nodded. 'I know. I felt just the same. I expect most people do. What comes next to this? The School Hall? My dear, what a magnificent place! This is lovely! Oh, why *am* I not young enough to go to school again?'

Joey laughed. 'I've felt like that off and on ever since I left school myself,' she confessed. 'But this last year it's not been so bad. For one thing, we haven't had the School, and that made a difference. For another, I think all that awful business of running away from the Gestapo definitely aged me. It did Bill—our science-and-geography mistress, you know. It turned her hair snow-white; and she had such glorious chestnutty hair before! You'll see her later. She and Hilda Annersley, the Head, are in Peterport, buying last-minute oddments. Con Stewart is with them. She teaches history. Then we have Mademoiselle Lachenais for languages, and my own chum, Simone Lecoutier, for maths. Miss Phipps has the babies; and Grizel Cochrane, who is another old friend, takes some of the music. Herr Anserl takes the stars. *And*,' Joey's voice became very impressive, 'our Matron is Matron Lloyd, who's been with us for years. It *was* a piece of luck getting Matey back. She'd gone to a big boys' school in the south of England. Then Nell Wilson wrote and told her we were opening here, and she presented her resignation, but she didn't expect to be able to come to us till after Christmas. However, the Head of the School had a sister who'd been training for Matron, and he wanted to give her the job, so he offered to release Matey at once, and no fuss. Come upstairs and meet her. She's in her room now.'

She led the way to a sunny room, where a small, wiry-looking woman looked up from her job of marking sheets, and welcomed Jo with a look that told Janie Lucy that here was 'Matey's' heart's dearest, though all she said was, 'Well, Jo! So you've brought me a visitor?'

'This is Mrs. Lucy, Matey. Two of her babes are coming here; and she has one or two more we shall hope for in due course.'

'And my nieces are coming, too,' said Janie, with her own grin. 'I do so hope you will be happy here, Matron. Guernsey is the apple of my eye, you know. You must come to us on your free day, and meet the younger members of my family, not to mention my little adopted sister, Nan Blakeney, and my lengthy husband.'

Matron replied amiably, and after a brief chat, Janie Lucy rose to take her leave. 'I've stayed ages, and I meant to make such a proper twenty-minutes' call. I'm going to call on your sister next week some time, Jo. I hear she's got a new daughter.'

'Not so very new—about ten months old now. Not nearly so new as your son. By the way, what's his name?'

'Barnabas. There's a story attached to it, of course.

He's a lamb, if it *is* his mother who says it. You'll love him. Do you like babies, by the by?'

'I've had to; our house is simply boiling over with babies of all ages. I couldn't have survived if I hadn't liked them. Bring Barnabas with you, and show him to Madge. If you'll ring me up, I'll come too, and inspect him. You can compare him with Josette.'

'What's your number, then? Shall I bring Nan? I'd like you to know her. She must be quite near you in age—she's nearly nineteen.'

'I'm twenty-one—that is, I shall be in November. Yes, do bring her; I love girls.'

'Right-ho. Put your number down on this, and then I'll ring you up, and you shall meet Barney and Nan. Come and have tea on Saturday-week, and see Betsy and Vi. Bring your husband, too, won't you?'

'Yes—if he can get away. They're rather full of the San, though,' said Joey, escorting her new friend down the drive. 'I rarely see Jack.'

'Is that his name? What a chorus of J's we shall be! My husband is Julian; I'm Janie; you're Joey; and now your husband is Jack!'

Joey chuckled. 'I expect we shall survive. Perhaps we could form a Jay Society among us. Madge's husband is Jem.'

'Don't say she's got a J in her names!'

'Oh, no; she's Margaret Daphne; and *my* little adopted sister is Marya Cecilia. We always call her Robin, though. Must you really go? Well, I'll see you soon. Goodbye!'

Joey watched Mrs Lucy as she set off down the road, and then returned to the house to find Robin and Daisy awaiting her, very reproachful that she had stayed away so long.

'Tomorrow we begin school,' said Robin, 'and then there won't be much time during the week.'

'Never mind,' said Joey comfortingly. 'You'll not be a boarder, you know, so we can see each other at night. Now come home. It's getting late, and I want my tea!'

CHAPTER XIV

THE FIRST DAY OF TERM

NEXT day there was great excitement at Les Rosiers, the new home of the Maynards, and also at Bonne Maison, the Russell abode. School began at nine. Everyone had to be there by ten to nine, and first bell would be rung then, second bell ringing at nine. Robin and Daisy were at Les Rosiers for the present, and were in such a hurry to get to school, that it was difficult for the elders to persuade them to eat an adequate breakfast.

By half-past eight the two schoolgirls were cycling down the road, leaving a regretful Joey behind. Halfway to school, they were passed by the Bonne Maison car, well loaded, and waved gaily.

They were early enough, as they found when they reached Sarres, when Robin was at once pounced on by Lorenz Maïco, who had arrived the previous evening.

'Oh, Robin! Isn't it fun to be going to the Chalet School again?' she cried, as she towed her friend to the Fifth Form cloakroom.

'Yes; but it's not quite the same,' said Robin. 'Where is my peg—next to you? Oh, good! How do you like it, Lorenz?'

'It is very nice, I think,' replied Lorenz, shaking back the long yellow pigtail that had fallen over her shoulder. 'I am in a dormitory with three others—Kitty Burnett, Polly Heriot, and Amy Stevens. There aren't more than four in any dormitory. The rooms are so much smaller than our old ones were. But it's rather nice to be so private, *I* think, though some of the others are grumbling.'

Robin finished hanging up her hat and changing her shoes before she answered. 'I would much rather be a boarder again. But they decided I'd better be at home. So Daisy and I are with Joey. It's a two-mile cycle ride, so we are staying for lunch—that's what you call Mittag-essen here,' she added, seeing that Lorenz looked puzzled.

'Oh, I see. Yes; we called Abendessen "supper" last night; and Frühstück this morning is "breakfast" now. And how is Joey, Robin? What is she like now she's married?'

'Just the same—or very nearly,' said Robin. 'Are we allowed to talk in the corridors, Lorenz?'

'Of course not! And not really in the cloakrooms. But as this is first day, Miss Annersley said we might. But we must keep to rules after today. Robin! Did you know that Maria Marani is Head Girl?'

'Yes—Joey told me. Has she come? Lorenz, is there any news of her father?'

Lorenz shook her head. 'Not a word. Frau Marani is in Paris, you know. She is to come to England to live with Gisela and Gottfried. Did you know that Gisela has a son, born two weeks after she left the Sonnalpe?'

'Of course,' said Robin. 'We've seen photos of him, and Madame saw him when she was in London three months ago.'

Lorenz looked at her friend admiringly. 'How well you speak English now, Robin! I suppose that's with being in England.'

Robin laughed. 'This isn't England, exactly. It's Nor-man French. But I haven't heard much but English since we left Tyrol, and it makes a difference.'

'Well, here's our form-room!' And Lorenz shepherded her into a sunny room where seven other girls of their own age were clustered together at the window. At sight of Robin, they raised a shout of welcome, and came to meet her.

'Robin! What fun to see you again! Oh! You're grow-ing your hair!' exclaimed a curly-headed person of fourteen, whose impish blue eyes and tip-tilted nose told a tale.

'Yes; they thought I might as well now,' explained Robin. 'How are you, everyone? It's jolly seeing you all after all this time!'

The first bell sounded at this moment and sent them

to their seats in a hurry, and when their form mistress entered, she found them all sitting awaiting her with demure faces. They rose at her entrance; but almost at once they forgot their demureness, and a shout arose.

'Simone! Simone Lecoutier! Have you come back to teach? Are you really our form mistress? Oh, what fun!'

Simone Lecoutier, a little, dark French girl, with very neat black head, and quick-glancing black eyes set in a small, sallow face, blushed at this vociferous welcome.

'Sit down, girls,' she said in rapid, fluent English—for, like all the girls who had been at the Chalet School, she was trilingual. 'Yes; I am your form mistress, and I am very glad to see you all again. But I've got to impress you with one thing. In school, at any rate. I'm afraid you mustn't call me "Simone." It would be bad for the Juniors and any new girls we may get. Do try to remember to say "Miss Lecoutier," or I shall have to give order-marks. Miss Annersley and Madame both say so.'

'How awful!' declared someone. 'I shall never remember.'

'You must try, Kitty,' replied Miss Lecoutier with some sternness, and Kitty Burnett was reminded of the time when Simone Lecoutier had been Second Prefect at the Chalet School, and a firm disciplinarian she had been. She proceeded to call over the names of the nine girls who constituted her form, and Robin noted that they were all old friends.

'Miss Lecoutier,' she said, 'are we all for the Fifth?'

Simone nodded. 'Yes; nine of you. And it is the largest form, so far,' she added. 'Don't look so upset, girls. I can remember when the Fifth Form at the Chalet School had only six girls in it. And when there was no Fifth Form at all, but only Senior, Middle, and Junior forms. Think back to your first year with us, Robin.'

'How many are there altogether. Si—Miss Lecoutier?'

'Fifty-two, Enid. But we hope to grow again presently.'

The Prayers bell stopped any further discussion, and Simone issued instructions. 'Protestant girls go to the

Kindergarten—you will see the name on the door. Catholic girls to the Art room at the far end of this passage. No more talking, girls. Remember you are one of the top forms now, and must set an example to the Juniors. Kitty Burnett, please lead the way to the Kindergarten.'

They marched off as they had been told, and the Protestants found that Prayers for them would be taken by Miss Annersley, the Head Mistress; while Miss Wilson, as Second Mistress, took the Catholics. It had always been arranged this way at the School, and there had been no trouble. When Prayers were over, they all marched into Hall, where they squatted on the floor while Miss Annersley gave them her beginning of term speech.

'I am very glad to welcome you back to the Chalet School, girls,' she began. 'We are a small School now. You all know what happened last year, and how we were dispersed. Now we must begin again. To us it is entrusted to build up our School once more. Let us see to it that we build well and truly.

'Madame gave us a watchword that last term at the Sonnalpe you may remember. It was "Be Brave." We may need to be very brave, and that very shortly. Let us take it for our motto for the first year of the new School. Let us "Be brave" as far as in us lies.

'Now I must turn to other things. We shall have Head Girl and Prefects, just as we have always done; and I have here their badges, so I will call on them to come up and get them. Maria Marani!'

Maria Marani, changed from the merry schoolgirl of eighteen months before to a very grave person, walked up through the files to the platform, and stood to have the Head Girl's badge pinned on her tunic. Nothing had been heard of her father for nearly a year, and there was grave reason to fear that he was dead. She was received with cheers, for she had always been a popular person, and she flushed slightly as she returned to her place; but she said nothing, and no smile came to her lips.

'Cornelia Flower,' called Miss Annersley. 'Cornelia is

105

Games Prefect, and will be seeing about her teams shortly.'

Cornelia, with a plait of bright hair down her back, wide blue eyes and a well-squared jaw, strode up to get her badge and returned to sit down by Maria and slip a consoling hand into hers.

'Violet Allison! And Violet will be responsible for the library—non-fiction branch.'

Violet, a shy, mousy person, who could, nevertheless, display unexpected force of character on occasion, crept through the ranks for her badge, and sat down again thankfully when the little ceremony was over. She preferred a quiet life with no publicity.

'Yvette Mercier, you are our magazine prefect, and, therefore, editor. Come along, dear.'

Yvette, a typically French girl, received her badge, and then the last of the prefects was called. This was Sigrid Björnesson, a Norwegian, and a cousin of Giovanna Rincini, who was now in a Woman's Labour Corps, the Nazis having given orders that all girls between the ages of seventeen and twenty-five who were unmarried were to join.

'Now for the form prefects,' said Miss Annersley. 'I will read out their names, and they will line up, and come up in a body. Fifth Form, Robin Humphries; Fourth Form, Biddy O'Ryan; Third Form, Daisy Venables; Second Form, Peggy Burnett; First Form, Nancy Chester; Kindergarten'—she flashed a smile at the tinies who were sitting just below her—'is Edmund Eltringham. Come along, little ones.'

They trotted up, headed by Robin, whose face was very serious, and ended by six-year-old Edmund Eltringham, who returned proudly to his place when the little silver badge had been fixed to his grey pull-over.

'You now know all the officials among yourselves,' said Miss Annersley. 'Today, the Staff will examine you in all subjects, and it may be that some of you will have to be moved up or down in your forms. We begin with the ordinary time-table on Monday. I forgot to say that we have one innovation. There is a great deal of ground here, and we shall not require it, at present at any rate, for playing-fields and buildings. We have therefore decided to give each form a garden, and Mrs Russell has promised a form prize for the garden that does best next summer. You may grow what you please, and you may ask advice of anyone. But you are to do all the work yourselves. The beds are already dug over, and fully prepared for planting. Now I think that is all. There is no school this afternoon, so all day-girls will go home at half-past twelve—twelve for the Junior School.—Thank you, Miss Cochrane.'

Grizel Cochrane, at the piano, struck up a march, and, beginning with the Kindergarten, the girls marched out to their form-rooms, where the various Staff came to them at once, for the Head's instructions had been that they must be kept in order till Break, which came at 10.30, when they were to have twenty minutes in which to discuss the new state of affairs thoroughly.

So it was not till Break, when they had all got their milk and biscuits in what was known as the house-keeper's room, and disposed of them and gone out into the garden, that they were able to talk. But then they certainly made up for lost time.

A select coterie from the Sixth gathered together near the rose arbour, a very earwiggy place which speedily became known as 'Sixth Form Harbour'—Enid, needless to say, was responsible for this piece of wit. The Fifth congregated round the enormous garden roller in one corner of the lawn, and Robin and Lorenz perched themselves on it, while Enid and Kitty took possession of the wheelbarrow that stood near. The rest piled on to a garden seat, and they held a meeting which was rowdy if nothing else.

'Well!' cried Enid. 'What do you all think of everything?'

'Do you realise,' asked Kitty impressively, 'that we—we—are almost Sixth now? We're Seniors. And when last we met we were only Senior Middles. I do feel so aged!' And she heaved a sigh.

'Well, but we aren't babies now, are we?' asked Robin.

107

'Fifteen, aren't we? Most of us, anyway. Fifteen is old enough to be Seniors.'

'I realise it a bit better when I look at you, Rob,' said Enid. 'Growing your hair has made you tons older. And, talking about hair, what d'ye think of Bill, anyone? Did you see how she glared at me? It was quite like old times!' And she sighed in an elderly manner.

'Well, you deserved it,' said Robin consideringly. 'Really, Enid, you can't chatter like that, now you're a Senior. Remember what the Abbess said. W've got to build up the new School, and we've all got to pull our weight. We shan't do that if you go fooling about.'

'Robin, I've never been really serious in my life. Do you expect me to begin at this advanced age?'

'Maria might have said that eighteen months ago,' said Lorenz abruptly.

Enid sobered at once. 'Is there *no* news of her father? How awful! One would almost rather know he was dead and be done with it.'

'Especially as if he isn't dead he must be in one of their horrible concentration camps,' said a bright-faced girl of their own age. 'Dad says the Middle Ages have nothing on the Nazis when it comes to torture.'

Amy Stevens' father was a well-known journalist, so these words carried weight with the girls.

'It's so ghastly—one feels so helpless,' said Enid, as grave as anyone could have wished to see her. 'There's absolutely *nothing* we can do, either. Poor Maria!'

'Yes,' said Robin. 'The Abbess told us to pray, and we *can* do that.'

The girls said nothing. They were shy of such talk, but each one vowed in her own heart that if prayer would do anything for Herr Marani, whom they had all known and liked, it would not be neglected. The bell rang then, and they had to return to their form-room, where they found pretty Miss Stewart waiting to show them which was their garden. Enid heaved a low sigh of relief. At least 'Charlie,' as Jo had christened her years ago, was unchanged!

After they had inspected the great bed set aside for

108

them, they returned to Mademoiselle Lachenais and French, and found that the long break had wiped a good deal of French construction from their memories, only Robin, Lorenz, and a French girl, Susanne Mercier, satisfying jolly little Mademoiselle during the talk that followed. Finally they had an English lesson with Miss Annersley, and then school ended for the day. They were told that on the morrow they would have tests in those lessons in which they had not already been tested. In the afternoon there would be games, when they would see about forming lacrosse and netball teams; and on Monday they would begin work at once.

'So endeth the first day of the new School!' remarked Enid as she was putting away her books in her locker. 'Robin, I wish you were still a boarder. Give my love to Joey and tell her to buck up and come and see us. I'm dying to see how much she has aged. Marriage is said to be a very ageing affair.'

CHAPTER XV

THE FOURTH CREATE A SENSATION

THE School settled down comparatively quickly. Hitherto, the Chalet School had been a boarding-school, with just an odd day-girl now and then. Now it was both day and boarding, with twenty of its members as day pupils. It is true that most of these were in the lower forms; but the Fifth had Robin Humphries; and the Third had Daisy Venables and Beth Chester. Robin was by way of being a power in the land, and Daisy and Beth were leaders in their form. They had struck up a great friendship, which was smiled upon by all concerned, for Daisy had no other friends in Guernsey; and Beth, coming from a school where the education was good enough of its kind, but the girls of a very different class, with an outlook on life of which her parents disapproved, had been almost as lonely. Consequently, her character had threatened to become warped.

Then the Chalet School had been opened, with the chance of a good education for Beth among girls of healthy outlook on life; and, best of all, this friendship with Daisy Venables. Beth was very grateful for the change, and, having never had a friend of her own age, 'adored' Daisy, who was a sensible little person, and was quite willing to be as chummy as anyone could wish.

With these two as leaders of the Third, that form was fairly safe for the moment. But it was different with the Fourth, which contained four of the naughtiest girls the Chalet School had ever known, and was further enlivened, when the term was only a week old, by the arrival of Betty Wynne-Davies, who, from the tip of her furthermost black curl to her pointed toes, was impudence and mischief incarnate. She, and Biddy O'Ryan, a wild Irish scamp, Elizabeth Arnett, of whom someone had once said, 'Elizabeth *thinks* of wicked things to do, and Betty *does* them—with frills on!', and Mary Shaw, a young American, made a good match and kept things going. The Chalet School had never had the reputation of being a specially peaceful place, and if the present Fourth had any say in the matter, it never would, so long as they were in it.

It began one day when they were gardening. Gardening was included in the lessons, for, as Miss Wilson had pointed out, it might be a vital matter to the nation. So one day in the week, each form spent at least two hours learning all about soils, and fertilisers, and the habits of various plants. In wet weather, they were to go in for cold-house work, potting, and other important details.

It was the Fourth Form's turn to be under the instruction of Miss Everett, the new young visiting mistress, who was gardener at Les Arbres, and who had taken a course at the great horticultural college at Swanley. She was, as I have said, young, keen, but rather impatient, especially so with people who did not see what she meant at once.

It had not taken Elizabeth Arnett three lessons to

realise this. She thought it over, and then summoned Betty Wynne-Davies and Mary Shaw for a confidential chat on the subject.

'Evvy's a bit of a tartar when she gets roused,' she said.

'We know that without being told, I guess,' said Mary, who had been in trouble at the last lesson for not planting winter spinach correctly. 'You haven't dragged us out here to tell us that, have you?'

'Don't be an idiot, Mary! Of course I haven't. But—I was thinking—we can't have quite the fun here that we used to have at the Tiern See. We must try some new things.'

'Well?' demanded Betty.

'Well, it's fun at the time to get Bill going, of course. And Charlie is even more fun. But it's not awfully safe. They have so many ways of getting back at one since they live at the School. Now Evvy only comes one day in the week. Julie Lucy told me that she's their head gardener, so of course she couldn't spare time for more. The worst she can do is to give us order-marks or lines, and they don't matter.'

'They do, though. If we get four order-marks it means being out of Saturday evening fun,' objected Mary. '*You* may not mind spending all your free time writing lines, but *I* do.'

'Oh, well, just be careful not to do things that mean lines or marks. But you're not a bit a sport, Mary!' said Elizabeth impatiently.

'Well, get on with what you want to say,' said Mary. 'I don't know a word of my Latin, and I don't want a deten. this afternoon if I can help it. I must give a squint at those horrid deponent verbs.'

'Well, all I was going to say was that it would be quite an idea to do a few things in gardening—say, mix seeds, to start with. Wouldn't Evvy get a shock if cabbages came up where she'd planted carrots or leeks?'

'You can't mix up cabbages and leeks,' objected Betty. 'Leeks are baby onions—at least, I *think* so,' cautiously.

111

'And I know you don't grow cabbages from seed. You buy cabbage plants.'

'And what do cabbage plants come from but seed?' jeered Elizabeth. 'Did you think you pulled them off old plants like geranium cuttings?'

'Well, *we* aren't growing them from seed, for Evvy said she was bringing the plants next week.'

'Oh, well, I was only giving them as examples. And carrots *do* grow from seed, anyhow. Can't we mix them with something?'

'We *might*, but I don't think it'd be much fun. We'd have to wait ages before they came up. And then it might turn out to be something she was thrilled to know was planted. If that's all you can think of, I think your brain's gone mushy.'

'Well, I'm going to get a squint at my Latin. I don't know it one mite, and Mademoiselle will go bats if she asks me any questions,' said Mary; and she left them still quarrelling about it.

That idea came to nothing; but a few days later, Miss Everett found that all the garden tools had been scattered. Two spades, a fork, and five hoes turned up. Someone found a couple of trowels in the rockery. But most of their implements were not to be found.

Sparks flashed from her hazel eyes. 'Who had them last?' she asked, an ominous calm in her tones.

'The Fifth,' came a chorus.

'Very well. Elizabeth and Betty, go on fixing the strings for those seed-lines. Biddy and Nicole, begin to dig at the first ones. Myfanwy, you can sprinkle the seed— very thinly, please—and Mary Shand may help her. The rest of you can rake the soil over as soon as the seed is sprinkled. Only lightly, mind. You don't want to give your spinach too thick a layer to grow through.' And she swung round and marched off to the house, indignation in every line of her figure.

The conspirators watched her with some alarm. They had never meant to bring the Fifth into it, and they knew that such people as Robin and Lorenz and Amy Stevens would be quite sharp enough to hit on the people responsible for the trouble. They had expected Miss Everett to be angry, but they hadn't expected her to take this line.

'Besides,' said Betty uneasily to Elizabeth as they carefully measured their spaces, 'the Abbess and Bill will be bound to hear of it, and—well—they're always so on the spot.'

Meanwhile, Miss Everett had gone straight to the formroom where the Fifth were having English literature with no less a person than the Head. When that lady heard the furious knock with which the gardening mistress heralded her arrival, she raised her eyebrows involuntarily. When, in answer to her 'Come in!' Miss Everett irrupted into the room, clearly as angry as she could well be, she hastily searched her memory of the time-table to find out who should be having a lesson with her.

Not that she showed this. Her quiet, 'Do you want me, Miss Everett?' showed nothing of what she was thinking.

'Yes, Miss Annersley!' cried Miss Everett. 'At least I want to know why the Fifth did not put away the garden tools when they had finished with them. Here am I, stopped in my work, and the tools probably lying out in the grounds rusting, just because girls of fifteen are such babies that they can't be trusted to put their own tools away!'

Miss Annersley turned to the form, which was sitting bolt upright, all surprised, and most of them as indignant as Miss Everett herself at this unfounded accusation.

'Robin, you are form prefect,' said the Head. 'When did you last use the tools?'

'Yesterday afternoon, Miss Annersley.'

'Where did you put them when you had finished with them?'

'In the tool-shed, Miss Annersley. Cornelia and Maria saw us,' added Robin. 'They were getting their bicycles from the cycle-shed next door, as they were going to have tea with Marie von Wertheimer, and Cornelia told us not to leave the spades stacked up because they would fall down at a touch, and might hurt someone. So we put them in a corner where they would be safe, and pulled the sawing-horse across.'

'Who is your class, Miss Everett?' asked Miss Annersley quietly.

'The Fourth, Miss Annersley.' Miss Everett was beginning to cool down a little, and saw that she had made a bad mistake. Being an honest if hasty person, she added, 'I'm sorry I accused you girls like that, without hearing your side, but I was annoyed at being delayed.'

'Oh, we all make mistakes,' said the Head quickly. 'I can understand that you are anxious to get on with the work. It is work for the nation, though I don't know if those wild scaramouches in the Fourth quite realise that. However, I will set these girls some work and come with you and make inquiries.'

She set some work, and the wildly indignant Fifth had to settle down to it as well as they could, while their mistress accompanied Miss Everett to the patch which the girls were engaged in turning into a kitchen garden. The Fourth saw them coming, and Betty promptly whistled with consternation.

'The Abbess herself! Oh, my stars! You've done it this time, Liz!'

Miss Annersley wasted no time. 'Who has hidden the tools?' she asked. Her gaze fell on the form's worst firebrands. 'Biddy, do you know anything about it?'

'Oi do not,' returned Biddy, becoming richly Irish at the question. She had begun life with a Kerry brogue like cream. Years at the Chalet School had largely cured her, but in moments of stress it bobbed up again.

Miss Annersley with a mere, 'Be careful of your English, please,' turned to the next person her eye fell on—Mary Shaw. 'What do you know about it, Mary?'

Now Mary had been with the other two when they had discussed the question of 'making Evvy mad,' though she had known nothing about the hiding of the garden tools. She therefore lost her head, and stammered, 'I didn't—I don't—I'm not sure—I think—I——'

Miss Annersley stopped her quickly. 'That will do,

Mary. Did you or did you not help to hide the garden tools?'

Faced with a plain question like this, Mary thankfully replied, 'No, Miss Annersley.'

The Head nodded. 'Very well. Go on with what you were doing, you two. Betty, do *you* know anything about it?'

Betty Wynne-Davies might be impudent and mischievous, but she was truthful. 'Yes, Miss Annersley,' she said.

'Ah! And did you help her, Elizabeth? I know it was more than one girl would be likely to attempt alone.'

'Yes, Miss Annersley,' replied Elizabeth sulkily.

'Quite so! Miss Everett, will you please excuse Betty and Elizabeth?'

'Certainly, Miss Annersley,' replied Miss Everett, casting a look of disfavour on the pair. 'But first may they tell us where to find the tools. All our work is being held up for lack of tools.'

'Of course. Be quick, you two, and tell Miss Everett what she wants to know.'

'They're everywhere,' said Elizabeth, still sulkily. 'Some of the spades are in the ditch, and the forks are in the shrubbery—'

Miss Everett interrupted her with a cry of dismay. 'Our beautiful tools among all that damp undergrowth? They'll be ruined! Run quickly, some of you—you, Faith, and you, Myfanwy—and find them. Where are the other things?'

Elizabeth told her. She and Betty, with an ingenuity worthy of a better cause, had contrived to scatter the tools broadcast, and, as the rest of the Fourth realised, the greater part of the gardening lesson would be taken up in hunting for them. Miss Annersley's face grew grimmer and grimmer as she heard the tale. When it was ended, she turned to Miss Everett.

'I see that this will cut completely into the lesson, Miss Everett. In the circumstances, I think the girls had better give up all attempt at gardening just now, and hunt up the tools. Then, instead of their netball practice at three o'clock, you can have them from three till five for a lesson. Will that be quite convenient to you?'

'Quite, Miss Annersley,' said Miss Everett, whose expression was now as grim as the Head's. 'If I may use the 'phone, I'll just let Mrs Lucy know that I shall not be round today at all. But I know she won't mind. And the children's nurse can call at my rooms when she takes them out this afternoon and explain that I shall not be home till six o'clock.'

'Very well. Betty and Elizabeth, go to the study, and wait there for me. The rest of you, go and bring the tools. Perhaps you would go to the shed, Miss Everett, and they can bring them straight there to you.'

The dismayed Fourth scattered to seek the tools, cursing Betty and Elizabeth freely in their hearts as they thought of their lost netball practice. Miss Everett departed to the tool-shed; and the Head went to deal with the culprits.

She soon reduced them to flinders. Reminding them that Britain was at war, and that the production of food was a matter of vital importance for the nation, she informed them that they could spend their spare time bringing the tools to their original state of silveriness. She awarded them a double order-mark apiece, said a few things about rudeness to a mistress, and then dismissed them to go to the shed and apologise for their stupid behaviour.

'Your own form will probably have a good deal to say to you also,' she added. 'That must lie between yourselves. And the Fifth will want to speak to you on the matter as well. However, when you so unpatriotically tried to stop the gardening, I expect you thought of all that. If you didn't you are even more stupid than I thought. Now run away, and please don't let me have you here again this term.'

They went; and if they had succeeded in their original idea of making Miss Everett angry, they found that the price they had to pay for it was a heavy one. Miss Everett accepted their apology; but it had rained overnight, and most of the tools, new that term, were badly rusted. It took all their spare time for the rest of the week to bring them back to the state of pristine freshness which alone satisfied Miss Annersley. Their own clan were furious at being docked of their netball, and told them what they thought of them in unmeasured terms. As for the Fifth, by the time those young people had finished with them, even Betty's cheeky nose looked depressed, which was a feat few people had managed to perform. All things considered, their joke had fallen remarkably flat.

CHAPTER XVI

THE NEW GIRL

'HEARD the news?' It was Enid who thus greeted Robin when that young lady was jumping off her bicycle one morning in early October.

War had been going on for some weeks now, and the girls were quite accustomed to war-time conditions, including black-out, which had been hard for those people who liked to have their curtains drawn back and their windows wide open at night. However, Miss Annersley had got over the difficulty by ordering the removal of all light bulbs from the dormitories, after lights-out, by whoever was on bed-time duty. The girls were allowed to have torches with blue-painted bulbs, and Matron and the Staff were similarly equipped. Downstairs, the huge cellars had been made into bomb-proof shelters, and one had been prepared as an anti-gas room. Gas-masks were taken wherever the girls went, and a good stock of tinned foods, water and earth for fire-fighting, and primus stoves and saucepans for emergency cooking, had been installed in various places.

In addition, the Senior time-table showed three lessons a week in elementary first-aid; and as all were Guides, they had taken to the lessons like ducks to water.

Robin put her bicycle away and took her satchel from the handle-bars before she replied to the question that Enid repeated excitedly.

'Only the eight o'clock news at breakfast time. Is there any more?'

'Oh—that! I didn't mean that! This is *School* news.'

'What is it?' Robin's thoughts flew to Maria Marani. 'Oh, is it that Onkel Florian is safe? Has word come?'

Enid's merry face sobered. 'I'm afraid not. Oh, I do wish they could hear one way or the other. Maria's getting so thin with worry. I'm sure she's not well, Rob, though she always says she is when you ask her. Couldn't you tell Dr Jem to come along and take a squint at her?'

'I expect he'll come when Matey sends for him,' replied Robin as they strolled to the house. 'Don't worry about Maria that way, Enid. Matey will keep an eye on her.'

'Well, I wish something would turn up. This waiting and not knowing is simply cruel!' said Enid vehemently. 'It's all very well for the Abbess to say we must feel no bitterness against the Germans, but when I think of Maria, I could kill the lot of them!'

'It isn't the Germans who are doing it,' said Robin. 'It's the Nazis. Joey says she thinks Hitler is Anti-Christ —from the Bible, you know. If he is, well, he'll come to a sticky end.'

'Let's hope he does—and before long, too!' said Enid uncharitably. Then she remembered her news. They must not talk, once they were in the house, so she caught Robin's arm and pulled her back from the door. "Don't go in yet, Rob. I want to tell you the news.'

'Well, hurry up, then. It's twelve minutes to, and I want to look over those wretched imports and exports of Japan. I don't know them—not to feel safe, anyhow.'

'Well, it's just—we have a new girl!' Enid stepped back and eyed her friend eagerly to know what she thought of it.

Robin was suitably excited. 'A new girl? At this time of the term? What a queer thing! What's her name; and which form is she in?'

'Her name is Gertrude Beck, and she's with us,' said Enid. 'Yes; isn't it weird? It's two weeks to half-term.'

'Why didn't she come sooner? Did she say?'

'No; only that it was arranged in a hurry. Bother! There's first bell! Hurry up and change, and come to our room and see her.'

Robin complied, and in about three minutes they were hurrying along to their form-room. Miss Lecoutier had an uncomfortable habit of being dead on time. This morning, however, she did not turn up till nearly nine o'clock. Miss Annersley had been holding a Staff meeting and none of the mistresses were on time. So Robin was able to make the acquaintance of the new girl and look over her own geography as well.

Enid hurried her friend into the form-room, and at once Amy Stevens turned round. 'Oh, *here* you are! — Gertrude, this is our form prefect—Robin Humphries. Robin, we've got a new member of form—Gertrude Beck. This is her.'

Robin came forward with a smile. 'Enid has just been telling me. When did you cross? I hope it was a good one. It can be *awful*!'

The new girl smiled. 'It was—not pleasant,' she acknowledged in a deep, musical voice which held certain intonations that set Robin frowning. It was not an English voice, though the English itself was fluent enough. But that mysterious thing called 'cadence' was un-English, though it was familiar enough to the form's prefect. She had heard it many a time at Briesau and the Sonnalpe—the voice of a German or Austrian girl. Even now Marie von Wertheimer's tones held something of it, though her small son was Yankee to the last note.

Robin murmured something, and looked at the new girl. Gertrude was an attractive person, with wavy brown hair, cut short, blue eyes, and a dimpling, rosy face. Her small features were modelled with a fastidiousness which called the word 'neat' to the fifth-former's mind. If there *was* a fault to find, it was that the set of the mouth was very hard for so young a girl. She could be no more than fifteen, and might even be Enid's age. That young woman, despite a harum-scarum personality, was exceedingly clever, and even brilliant on occasion. She was much the youngest girl in the form, most of them being well on in their fifteenth year, while she was just fourteen before term began.

Robin added a few more words of welcome, inquired if someone had seen that Gertrude had everything she required, and then sat down to do what she could with those tiresome exports and imports.

She was so deep in them that she almost forgot to rise when at last the door opened, and Miss Lecoutier came in. The mistress looked very white, and rather dazed. She went to her seat with a curt 'Good morning, girls!' and sat down to take register as briefly as possible. Her form exchanged glances with each other. What *was* the matter? Simone Lecoutier had once been a very emotional person, but her years at the Chalet School had taught her self-control, and she seldom showed what she felt nowadays. Something bad must have happened to make her look like that!

With her mind on school things, Robin jumped to the conclusion that the worst news about Herr Marani had come, but when they went to Prayers, Maria looked just the same. When Prayers were over—and the girls noted with interest that 'Bill,' too, looked upset—they were told to go to Hall as Miss Annersley wished to see them. Greatly wondering, for the Head rarely called the School together except for very important announcements, preferring to make the smaller affairs known in form, they marched into Hall, and found the rest of the School waiting for them. And all the Staff wore the same look. What *could* have happened? More; Miss Lecoutier, having seen them in, vanished, and did not take her accustomed place on the dais.

When the last of them was settled down, the Head spoke in a voice that was strained and hard, though she had it well under control.

'Girls, great sorrow has come to us as a school,
120

Mademoiselle Lepattre died early yesterday morning. The news reached me this morning.'

She paused, while a low murmur rose from all over the Hall. All the elder girls, with the sole exceptions of Beth Chester anrd Gertrude Beck, had known and loved Mademoiselle, who had been Head of the Chalet School for five years, having joined Madge Russell, then Madge Bettany, when it was first opened. After the latter's marriage, Mademoiselle had remained on as Head, and it was only when her own terrible illness of two years before had ended in complete invalidism for her that the School had given up any idea of her returning to them. Mademoiselle was Simone Lecoutier's second cousin, and had done much for both her and her younger sister. She had given them their education at the School; and had paid for Simone's training at the Sorbonne. Renée Lecoutier was musical, and when the School had broken up, she had gone to the Paris Conservatoire, and Mademoiselle had taken that, too, on her shoulders. So no one was surprised that Simone was upset.

The enforced journey from Tyrol had tried Mademoiselle highly; but once she was in France, she had seemed to recover a little, and many of the girls had been planning to spend Easter in Paris and see her again before war had broken out. Now she was gone—and so suddenly. They could not grasp it.

A queer sound from the corner where the Sixth were sitting made Miss Wilson spring forward, just in time to catch the Games Captain as she fell. Cornelia Flower had been motherless since her babyhood, and Mademoiselle had supplied the place of that mother as much as she could. The Games Captain was an unsentimental being, but she had given her kindly Head Mistress a deep love that no one except, perhaps, Jo, quite realised. Certainly Miss Annersley had not known of it, or she would have sent for Cornelia, and broken it to her more gently. As it was, she could only wait till Miss Wilson and Matron had carried the fainting girl away, and then she went on, still in that hard tone of voice.

'Mademoiselle had not been so well this past week. The

day before yesterday she complained of pain, and they sent for the doctor. When he came, he saw at once that it was only a question of a few hours. He was able to relieve her pain, and she never regained consciousness. Early this morning Mme Lecoutier 'phoned me that she died at half-past eight yesterday. We may be thankful, girls,' went on the Head gravely. 'Mme Lecoutier told me that if she had lived, she must have suffered very greatly. As it is, she has been spared it, and they are spared the grief of seeing her suffer. There will be a Requiem Mass said for her in our own little chapel to-morrow, and all who wish to attend may do so. Now that is all. I have only one more thing to say. Miss Lecoutier is very much upset, naturally, and I wish you all to spare her as much as possible. I have asked her to stay out of school, but she says that she would rather continue with her work, and she knows it is what Mademoiselle herself would have wished. Now will you go quietly to your form-rooms, please.'

The girls dismissed in almost dazed silence. They had loved Mademoiselle very dearly. She was middle-aged, plain, a stern disciplinarian; but she had always been just and fair. When anyone was in trouble, she had been sympathetic, and they knew that her whole life was bound up in the School she had helped to establish. It seemed impossible that she could be dead!

Simone was not in the Fifth Form when the girls entered, so they sat down and talked very quietly among themselves. Gertrude Beck looked from one to the other with puzzled eyes.

'I do not understand,' she said, addressing Robin. 'Who, then, is this Mademoiselle Lepattre that you are all so troubled at her death?'

Robin swallowed a lump in her throat before she replied. 'She was Madame's partner, and our Head after Madame married.'

'And who is Madame?' demanded the new girl.

'She owns the School,' said Enid, seeing that Robin was not far from tears. 'She began it, and she's always been a partner in it. Mademoiselle was the other partner.'

'But I thought Miss Annersley was Head Mistress?'

'So she is. But Madame and Mademoiselle own the School.'

'And you are so grieved for a teacher? I do not understand at all.'

'You didn't know Mademoiselle,' said Lorenz Maïco, speaking curtly. 'We have all lost a dear friend.'

Gertrude's blue eyes were still puzzled; but just then the door opened, and Miss Lecoutier came in quietly. She was still very white, but she taught with all her usual vigour, and the girls worked like Trojans, even Suzanne Mercier, whose strong point was *not* mathematics, putting her whole heart into her work. No one said anything, for no one quite knew what to say. Besides, they were old enough to see that the mistress was putting a terrific strain on herself to retain her self-control, and they were afraid of upsetting her.

Gertrude soon proved that she was good at maths. And when Mademoiselle Lachenais came to them for French, she showed herself fluent and well-taught, though her accent was inclined to be guttural. Bill came to them after that for geography, and again the new girl turned out to be quite level with her present form. Altogether, it seemed likely that she would stay with them.

When Break came, they wandered out to the garden, for it was a fine sunshiny day. The Sixth were in Sixth Form Harbour as usual. The Middles were in the shrubbery, walking quietly about in twos and threes. The Fifth congregated about their roller, and tried to make the new girl feel at home.

She was greatly interested in what they felt for Mademoiselle, and asked sundry questions about the old Chalet School which most of them were eager to answer. Only Robin held her tongue, and the rest, thinking that Mademoiselle's death was still in her thoughts, left her alone. But suddenly, she roused herself up as she heard Gertrude saying, 'So you had a number of Austrian and German girls among you? I wonder what were their names? For perhaps I may know some of them. I have lived in Germany most of my life. My father was at the Heidelberg University.'

'They have left now,' said Robin, speaking with sudden authority. 'It is of little use to recall their names. There goes the bell! We must go in now.'

She slipped her hands through the arms of Lorenz and Amy, and held them back while the rest hurried Gertrude to the house, explaining that rules must be kept perfectly today, at least.

'Why does this girl ask so many questions?' she asked of her two friends. 'I don't like it. Listen, you two! Get hold of the others and warn them to say nothing about Mario—d'you understand? And see that she gets nothing out of the Middles, either.'

'What on earth *for*?' gasped Amy, stopping dead in her surprise.

'Oh, *Amy*!' Exasperation sounded in Robin's voice. 'You know that we have no word yet of what's happened to Onkel Florian. I'm sure Gertrude is a German—I shouldn't be surprised if she really spelt her name without the last E. The Nazis have spies everywhere. It might make things ever so much worse for Onkel Florian if he should be in a concentration camp—and we don't know that he isn't—if it got known that his daughter was here, in an English school.'

'But then so is Gertrude,' objected Lorenz.

'That may be a very different thing. If she's been pushed on us as a spy, it would be all right for her. But Onkel Florian hated the Nazis and all their ways. And now, come on before Enid or Kitty can tell more than they ought. They've both of them got long tongues. We don't want Maria to have any more trouble than can be helped.'

They rushed in, and were just in time to reach the room before Miss Annersley herself arrived for their Shakespeare lesson.

That afternoon was free for Robin, so when half-past twelve came, she gathered her books together, and sorted them out carefully. Gertrude, standing near, watched her.

'You do not stay this afternoon?' she asked.

Robin looked up. 'No; this is a free afternoon. You will have prep till three, and then go for a walk till half-past four. After that, you will have tea, and then prep again till six. Then you do what you like. Get Amy and Lorenz to explain about the Hobbies Club to you. We hold it in the evenings, so I can't come except just occasionally, now that we have black-out. But Daisy and I do what we can at home.'

'Daisy? Who is she? Your sister?'

Robin thought carefully. 'She's a—a sort of cousin,' she said at last, for to explain the very complicated relations would have been something of a task. 'We live with my sister, Jo Maynard. She lives at Les Rosiers, out at Torteval. Haven't you seen Daisy? She's in the Third Form.'

'I'll look out for her,' promised Gertude.

Robin made up her mind to warn Daisy to say nothing about the Sonnalpe. Then she decided that the best plan would be to go to the prefects at once, and warn them about Gertrude. She didn't like the prospect, for she could scarcely say anything to Maria; and Cornelia was in bed as a result of her fainting-fit. She thought the prefects over in her mind. Yvette would probably laugh at her. Violet hated takiing the lead in anything, being a very shy person. There remained Sigrid. Sigrid hated all Nazis for her cousin's sake. No one knew what she might not do if she thought Gertrude one of them. And Robin was not sure.

'And I can't go to the Staff—not today,' she thought desperately. 'Anyway, I doubt if they'd believe me. Who *shall* I ask?'

As if in answer to her question, the door of the locker-room opened, and a girl came in—Polly Heriot of the chestnut locks and long chin.

With a gasp of relief that was almost a sob, Robin caught hold of her arm. 'Oh, Polly! I'm so glad you've come!'

Polly looked down at the small person with the two big bows tying back her shoulder-length curls, and saw deep trouble in the beautiful eyes. She set her books down on a nearby table, and slipped an arm round the younger girl's shoulders.

'What's wrong, Robin? Is it—Mademoiselle?' She dropped her voice on the last word. Polly had not known Mademoiselle very well, for her first half-term at the Chalet School had been mademoiselle's last. But she had liked what she did know, and guessed how the death of the late Head Mistress must affect anyone who had known her for so many years. She was greatly surprised, therefore, when Robin shook her head.

'Oh, no; I've nearly forgotten—*that*, I've been so worried.'

Polly removed her arm, walked over to the door, slamming it shut, and bolting it. Then she came back. 'Sit down, old thing. You're nearly all in. That's better. Now tell me what's wrong.'

Sitting in the one chair the room had, Polly kneeling by her, an arm round her, Robin poured out all the story of the new girl, and what she suspected.

'So long, at any rate, as we don't *know* whether Onkel Florian is dead or alive, nothing must be said that could make things worse for him,' she said desperately. 'How can we stop it, Polly?'

Polly judged that if Gertrude really were put into the School by the Nazis as a spy, they would know that Maria was there; but she knew better than to say so to Robin, who was obviously on the verge of a breakdown. Also, she made up her mind, then and there, that Herr Marani must be dead now. However, her first job was to calm the younger girl.

'If Gertrude really is a spy,' she said slowly, 'I think they've wasted a fearful lot of energy and money and so on for nothing. How could she ever get news into Germany? You're forbidden to send postcards, or photos, or printed matter at all to enemy countries. And anyway, if she did write to Germany, the Abbess would see the address and want to know all about it. She has to be

126

'extra careful, of course, because this is a school.'

'She probably won't write to Germany at all,' replied Robin. 'She would know it wouldn't be any use. But what she *could* do would be to write to someone in England, and they could pass on the news. And you know yourself, Polly, that they have the weirdest ways of getting news across there.'

'They certainly *broadcast* the weirdest news! ' said Polly; for at this time, Germany was vehemently insisting that a U-boat had sunk the *Ark Royal*, despite repeated denials from the Admiralty. 'Yes; I see what you mean. Look here, Rob, I think the best thing will be for me to go to the Abbess and tell her what you think. Then she can do what she thinks best about stopping anyone talking of Tyrol. You know, there are lots of girls here who would think it no harm to tell a new girl all about— oh my stars! *The Chalet School League!* If this girl is a Nazi she simply mustn't hear of it—or not until we've had time to convert her. Look here! I'll go to the Abbess. And you get off home, and tell Jo. She may be able to think up something. She's got us out of a good many holes at once time or another. Leave your books. You aren't likely to do much good with them today. I'll tell the Abbess I told you to do it. Listen! There's Daisy ringing her bell off for you. Off you go, and don't worry any more. I'll see to it; and you tell Jo, and among us all we'll manage something.'

'Yes; but I *can't* tell Jo,' returned Robin, despair in her tones.

'Why on earth not?'

'Because Jem says Jo isn't well just now and isn't to be excited or worried.'

Polly's eyes widened, and she rounded her lips to a soundless whistle. 'Oh? Well, if Jo isn't to be worried or excited, I'd advise you to take that look off your face before you see her again. She'll know there's something up the minute she sees you if you don't. And she'll soon ferret out what it is. You ought to know Jo by this time! '

Poor Robin looked as if she would burst into tears on

the spot. Mut Daisy produced such a frantic fantasia on her bicycle-bell at this moment that she took Polly's advice about her homework; she tumbled her books into her locker, and hurried off, scarcely taking time to thank the elder girl for her help.

Left alone, Polly disposed of her own load, and then went to the study to seek Miss Annersley and lay everything before her.

CHAPTER XVII

GERTRUDE STARTLES THE SCHOOL

LUCKILY for Robin, Joey set down that young lady's obvious trouble to Mademoiselle's death. She, herself, was not so upset. She had known something of the late Headmistress's suffering, and amid her grief for their own loss, she felt gladness that all pain was over now. No one could wish Mademoiselle back to suffer as she had done. They could only be thankful that she was at peace.

The tiny private chapel at the Chalet School, built for the many Catholic girls who were members, was filled to overflowing for the Requiem. All the doctors from the Sanatorium attended, for they had all known and admired the dead woman, who had borne tortures with such courage. Mrs Chester, Mrs Ozanne, and Mr and Mrs Lucy, with their adopted sister, Nan Blakeney, also came, and the entire School was present—including Gertrude Beck, who watched the proceedings with an air of superiority which surprised those who knew nothing of Robin's surmises. Polly Heriot also watched her, and became convinced that the younger girl was right in what she had guessed.

'That girl's a Nazi, or I'm a Dutchman,' she thought. 'What on earth is she grinning over it like that for?

I wonder what the Abbess will do? It's going to be a bit difficult, I should think.'

The next day the School returned to its normal activities, for, as the Head told them, that was what Mademoiselle herself would have wished. And still Miss Annersley made no sign.

On the Friday of that week, Gertrude, finding herself with a free period, since she did not take Latin (which she had never learnt), decided to make the acquaintance of some of the younger ones. It had been decided that, for the present, the School should not continue its House system. But each of the three divisions—Senior, Middle, and Junior—had its own common-room. They took their walks apart, for the Seniors were accustomed to long tramps of five and six miles at a time, which the tinies, at any rate, could not have managed. As for the Middles, they had no wish to mix with their elders, of whom they saw enough in school hours. They went off, with their own duty mistress, by themselves and had glorious times in Vazon Bay, Cobo Bay, and right round to Pleinmont, where Beth Chester, brought up on the old Guernsey legends, enlivened the walks by relating them. Her aunt, Mrs Ozanne, had published a small book of the said legends years before; and her own mother, an artist of no mean accomplishments in the days before the troubles came, had painted pictures from them. Therefore Beth knew her subject well, and she alternately thrilled her hearers and, to quote Betty Wynne-Davies, 'made their spines curl' with the horrors she related.

Evenings were mostly given up to prep, practice, first-aid, and preparing for the bazaar the School had always held at the end of the Easter term to provide a free bed or beds at the Sanatorium. So Gertrude had not had much chance of coming across her juniors.

On this occasion, the Middles were enjoying a free period, too, and were making the most of it in the garden, where they were flying about, shrieking at the tops of their voices, and generally letting off steam. The Chalet School believed in giving its girls a good deal of freedom, and as no neighbours were near enough to be

129

E

annoyed, the Third Form might enjoy itself as it chose, so long as it did no damage and refrained from killing anyone.

Gertrude put on her blazer, changed her shoes in obedience to rules, and strolled out into the October sunshine. It was quite warm—it is seldom really cold in Guernsey—and as she went down the path, the sun shining on her brown hair and bringing out golden lights in it, she almost wished that she had nothing to do but enjoy this delightful place. Then she set her lips and squared her shoulders. She had been sent here on a mission—a mission for the Führer and Greater Germany; she must accomplish it, and not be so selfish as to think of her own pleasure. At home, in Germany, she knew that her cousins and friends were living only just this side of starvation, while she was revelling in good food. Until she came here, she had not tasted milk for nearly two years. Eggs had been a great luxury, and as for the meat dishes which they had six days in the week at their mid-day meal, they were a treat which Gertrude thought she could not sufficiently enjoy. And there were sweets and cakes, too, though not so many as she would have liked. Gertrude was frankly greedy about sweet things, probably as the result of having been deprived of them for so long.

She had all this, and she must make some return for it. At the same time, the friendliness and kindness which were offered her gave her a strange feeling of meanness that she had never known before. It is true that she had been taught that spoiling the enemy was only the right thing to do, especially in wartime. But somehow she couldn't feel about it as she had expected. Still, it was her business to try to find out what it was that these girls had been so nearly caught hiding in the mountains round the Tiern See, and she must do it. She had not got much from her own form. They, warned by Lorenz, had given very little away. The Sixth were inclined to stand on their dignity, and when she had tried to get something out of Ruth Wynyard and Polly Heriot as being the most approachable of the seven, they had both turned the chatter, and in such a way that she could scarcely start the subject again. She had been warned to be very careful, lest anyone should suspect her nationality and object, so she had let the matter drop. However, it was unlikely that children of eleven and twelve would manage so well.

She ran down the grassy bank on to the former bowling-green, and found herself among six girls who promptly stopped running and screaming to stare at her wide-eyed.

'Did you want anything, Gertrude?' asked one of them politely, and Gertrude recognised Daisy Venables, the form prefect.

'Oh, no,' she replied pleasantly. 'But I have a free period now, and I felt rather lonely, so I came to see what the fun was.'

'Just cross tag,' said a young person with a mop of chestnut curls flying round her and deep violet eyes full of laughter. 'Would you like to join?'

'If I may. It looks great fun, and I've never played it.'

All talking together, they explained to her the principles of the game, and if Gertrude thought somewhat scornfully that it was a baby's game, she said nothing but joined in, and presently found that she was really enjoying it with all her might. It did not seem worth while to bother with her mission at the moment. Far better get these girls to grow friendly, and she would stand a better chance of finding out what she wanted to know. So Gertrude put in the rest of the period in rushing about, chasing and being chased, and returned to her form-room with rosy cheeks and somewhat tumbled hair, but ready for the work again.

The Third, on their side, had been charmed with the new girl, and eagerly welcomed her to their game next time she came. This went on for a fortnight. Then Gertrude, urged thereto by a letter which came from England, but originally came from a much greater distance, began to feel her way.

'How long have you been here?' she asked Daisy Venables when she caught her alone one day.

'Oh, not quite two years,' said Daisy carelessly.

'Oh, I did not mean in Guernsey,' said Gertrude, laughing, 'but in the Chalet School. It was in Austria-Tyrol, was it not?'

'Oh yes. Auntie Madge started it there,' replied Daisy. 'I didn't know you meant that, Gertrude. I've been four years at school. Before that, we lived in Australia, in Queensland. But that was when—when Mummy was alive,' she added with a gulp.

Gertrude was not interested in the whole of Daisy's past, but the gulp touched her rather hard little heart. If she *had* a soft spot, it was for her mother; and she knew, for Robin had mentioned it, that Daisy and Primula were only recently motherless. So she said in gentler tones than usual, 'It's hard for you, Daisy. Primula is too little; but you are old enough to miss her dreadfully. I know how I should feel if anything happened to *my* mother.'

Daisy looked up, and met the genuine sympathy in the blue eyes. She felt drawn to Gertrude as a result. 'Auntie Jo says it would be wrong to fret and wish her back, for she had such a hard time; and now she has got our little brothers again, and she's never tired or unhappy. But sometimes—in bed—it does seem so hard not to have her with us.'

'I know,' said Gertrude, still gently. 'But if she had such a hard time, it would be selfish to bring her back here. But I am sorry for you, Daisy. I love my mother, too, so dearly.'

Yes; and if she failed in her mission, trouble might recoil on the head of that beloved mother. Gertrude was old enough to know that the Nazi régime is utterly ruthless. She shivered, though the sun was warm, and paled a little as she thought of it.

Daisy noticed it. 'Are you cold? But you must have *taken* cold if you are. It's almost as hot as summer today.'

'Just a sudden idea that scared me,' replied Gertrude with a forced smile. 'Let's talk of something else. It wasn't a nice idea. Tell me about the School when it was in Tyrol. Where was it exactly?'

'At Briesau, on the Tiern See,' said Daisy. 'And part of it was at the Sonnalpe beside the San. Uncle Jem started that, you know.'

'I don't quite understand. How part of it at the Sonnalpe?'

'That was for girls who weren't strong. My little sister was there just the last term. So was I, if you come to that. The School was moved up to the Sonnalpe after the Anschluss. It was such a surprise! We went away for half-term—I went to stay with Onkel Reise in Innsbruch—and when we came back, instead of walking up the mountain-path to Briesau, there were motor-buses, and we drove up the coach-road to the Sonnalpe, and there the School was in a big hotel. I forgot, though. That wasn't the last term. That was the Easter term. The last term finished in June, when the Nazis ordered the School to close. That was because Auntie Joey and some of the others tried to help poor old Herr Goldmann the jeweller when some little pigs tried to kill him because he was a Jew. They did save him then; but the beasts went back to his house later, and killed him and Frau Goldmann. They shot Vater Johann at the church, too, because he helped our girls to escape somehow. Bill was there, too. That's when her hair went white.'

At this point Polly Heriot came running through the shrubbery where the pair were, and seeing Daisy with the elder girl, she interfered at once. 'Daisy Venables! Where have you been? Do you know the time?'

Daisy glanced down at the watch which had been the pride of her heart since Joey and Jack had given it to her on her thirteenth birthday. 'It says three minutes to two! I'll be late for the walk!' she gasped, and she turned and shot off towards the house, where Beth was calling for her impatiently.

Joey was unable to take long walks at present, so it had been arranged that Robin and Daisy should stay every afternoon, and go with their forms. As a result, Beth had begged leave to do the same, and Dr Chester had given in. The trio stayed to tea, which was at four, and then set off for home at once, thus arriving well before black-out just now, though the elders were saying that when summer-time came to an end, something else must be arranged.

Left alone with Gertrude, Polly looked at her. 'Don't keep Daisy past time another day, Gertrude,' she said. 'She'll get into trouble if she's late, you know.'

'I didn't mean to,' said Gertrude, 'but she had been talking of her mother, and I tried to comfort her a little and make her think of something else.'

Polly's keen grey eyes softened at this. 'That was kind of you. Jo Maynard says that Daisy still frets for Mrs Venables very badly at times. She was old enough to know what she lost, you see.'

'I know,' said Gertrude curtly. 'I—I should break my heart if anything happened to *my* mother. She's all I've got now.'

'Then you've more than I have,' remarked Polly. 'I haven't a soul in the world—except my Guardian, and he's old, though he's a perfect dear. Are you going back for prep? Come along, then.'

They strolled back to the house, Polly, in answer to Gertrude's questions, explaining that she had lost her parents when she was a baby, and had been brought up by great-aunts till their deaths when she was thirteen. 'Then my Guardian took me to Tyrol, and we—met—the School at Briesau, and I've been here ever since,' she concluded.

Gertrude said nothing. For one thing, they had reached the house and were entering the door, and silence in the passages and on the stairs was a strict rule. For another, she was again conscious of the queer feeling of shame over the part she was playing. She almost thought that if she had had only herself to consider, she would have dropped it. But there was her mother. Gertrude had a wholesome fear of the Gestapo activities, and she knew that even such an insignificant being as herself was marked by them.

At the door of the Sixth Form, she and Polly parted, and she went to do her best with algebra, science, French prose, and history. It was not a good best today. Her mind was too busy with other things, and the results of her prep brought trouble on her head at the next lessons in those subjects. Meanwhile she realised that she had set up a bond between herself and Daisy, and, for the sake of her mother, she decided to find out what she could from the younger girl.

For some days she got no chance. Polly privately warned Robin and Lorenz, and it seemed to Gertrude that whenever she was about to carry off Daisy Venables for a walk and talk, someone seemed to want her; or else they were joined by someone else.

Then her chance came. Daisy had talked of Gertrude at home, and finally asked leave to have her to tea. Joey, easy-going, and knowing nothing of what Robin suspected, granted it at once.

'Ask her by all means. You'll have to amuse her yourself, though. Rob is going over to Bonne Maison for the afternoon, and taking Lorenz and Amy with her. I'll write a note to the Head asking leave for Gertrude, and you can give it to her to-morrow. Are you sure she'll want to come? She's older than you, isn't she?'

'Yes; but she's jolly nice to me, Auntie Jo. I'd like to have her if it's only once, just as a return.'

'Oh, all right, then. Come for the note before you go to school in the morning,' said Jo, who was having breakfast in bed at present.

Later on, when Daisy had gone happily to bed, she asked Robin, 'Rob, what is this new girl in your form like? Daisy seems to have taken a violent fancy to her. I've said she can have her to tea on Saturday.'

It was Robin's chance if she dared have taken it. But she dared not. She remembered what Jem Russell had said about not worrying Jo, and she knew that any hint that Gertrude was a Nazi would have worried Jo considerably. So she only replied that Gertrude seemed all right, but that out of form she had very little to do with her. Joey, knowing that Robin had her own three chums, Lorenz, Amy, and Enid, thought no more about it, but wrote the note, and handed it over to Daisy when

135

that young person came to her room to say goodbye next morning.

'There's your note. I expect it'll be all right. Mind the coffee!' For Daisy, in the excess of her gratitude, had flung her arms round her, and the coffee-pot was sliding dangerously. Daisy righted it, and then kissed her aunt more quietly.

'Thank you ever so, Auntie. You are a dear! And you'll have tea with us on Saturday, won't you? Gertrude wants to see you so much.'

'Let's hope she's impressed by what she sees, then,' quoth Jo laconically. 'There's Rob raising the place for you. Scoot, my child, or you'll be late, and the Abbess may refuse to let Gertrude come.'

Daisy 'scooted' on the word, and found Robin waiting with both bicycles ready. 'Do hurry up, Daisy! What were you doing? We shall be late if you dither like this every morning.'

'I was only saying goodbye to Auntie Jo,' said Daisy cheerfully.

The pair mounted and rode off in silence at first. Then Robin decided to talk. 'Daisy, I want to say something to you.'

'Carry on, then. What is it?'

'Well—it's just that I want you to promise me to say nothing to Gertrude about the Chalet School League— not at present, at any rate.'

Daisy turned a genuinely startled face to the elder girl. 'Why ever not. Why shouldn't I talk about it to Gertrude?'

'Yes,' said Robin. 'But I think perhaps that had better come from someone in her own form or one of the Sixth. Promise me, Daisy, and say nothing at all about it.'

'I don't see why you should be so keen,' said Daisy. 'Oh, I'll promise, but I simply don't understand.'

'I'll talk it over with you later on,' promised Robin. 'There is no time just now. We must put on speed, or we'll be horribly late.'

So though Gertrude duly came to tea, and had her

afternoon alone with Daisy, she was no wiser in the end. Daisy would talk of the Chalet School when it had been down at Briesau; but she refused to say a word about it after that. She even shuddered when pressed.

'That was a horrid time. I don't want to think about it,' she said.

At tea, Gertrude was on her best behaviour, and rather took Jo's fancy, though, like Robin, Jo noted the faint intonation which told her that the girl was of German birth. However, there were plenty of non-Nazis in England, and she was far too busy with her new book to give more than a third of her mind to the affair, and it slipped her memory almost at once. After tea she played games with the two until it was time for Gertrude to cycle home, which had to be at six, and so the visit passed off.

But the leaven of the Chalet School atmosphere was working more and more strongly in the German girl. She noted how careful the girls were to speak as kindly as they could about her country. She saw how they did everything in their power for peace, hushing the younger ones when they talked about 'horrid Germans,' and, by word and deed, setting an example in tolerance that could not fail to have an effect.

At length, one day a letter came for the Nazi girl. She shivered when she saw it, for she knew that it meant more instructions, more urging along the path she was daily growing more and more unwilling to take. She received it from Miss Wilson with an inward shudder, and put it into her blazer-pocket, resolving not to open it until after morning school. She would have those few hours in peace, anyhow.

Her form were amazed at her this morning. She had never seemed so bright and witty. She was full of mischief, fastening one of Suzanne Mercier's long black plaits to the back of her chair with a drawing-pin. Suzanne, rising to take her work to Miss Lecoutier, found her chair come with her, and uttered a faint shriek of dismay. The rest stuffed their handkerchiefs into their mouths to stifle their giggles, for Suzanne's face of horror

137

struck them as one of the funniest things they had ever seen.

When 'Bill' after one of her usual thorough geography lessons had departed, leaving them for a few minutes alone, and Miss Annersley, who came to them next, was closeted with a visitor, Gertrude possessed herself of the chalk, and proceeded to turn the map of Australia, which Miss Wilson had sketched on the blackboard to illustrate the configuration of the continent, into the cottage of the Seven Dwarfs. She cleverly turned the outlines of the contours and the rivers into the dwarfs, and added Snow-white with a basket at her feet—Tasmania.

Of course Miss Annersley came in and caught her, but she did not drop on her with undue severity. She was wise enough to know that girls must have an outlet somewhere, and this was harmless, if rather cheek.

But, spin it out as she might—and *did*—Gertrude had to face that letter at last. Waiting till after lunch and their rest time, she at length took it from her pocket and opened it. It was reproach for the meagre information she had been sending; a hint that unless better news came from her, there would be penalties ahead. Finally, a demand to know what had become of her mother who had disappeared during the past week.

With a low cry of horror, the girl crumpled the letter, and lay almost rigid with fear. What had happened? Why had her mother disappeared? It had nothing to do with the police this time, for it was they who were asking her whereabouts. Oh, what could have happened?

Thankful that she had dropped her cubicle curtains and that, therefore, no one could see her, Gertrude turned her face to the pillow and lay very still, thinking.

One thought obsessed her. She must get back to Germany and find out her herself what had happened. She could stay here no longer. The trouble would be to get away. Once she had reached the continent—it must be by Denmark, she decided—she had enough money to get her to Heidelberg. What she would do there, if her mother had really vanished, she did not pause to consider. But she must get away, and that at once. During the whole rest period, she lay planning ways and means. She spent most of her preparation time over it as well, and by the time the gong sounded for tea, had everything settled. She knew of a Nazi who was living quite unsuspected, at Petit Bôt. She knew that he could help her, and she must impress on him somehow that she had been summoned back to Germany. Once that was done, the rest would be fairly easy. This arranged, she went off by herself after tea, and pretended to be busy with the kitchen garden. No one else joined her as it happened, the others preferring to work at their form beds.

The result was that when nine o'clock came, and she had not turned up all the evening, Lorenz, as sub-prefect of the form, reported to Miss Stewart, the mistress on duty, that Gertrude Beck was missing. A search was instituted, and fastened to her pyjamas they found, at long last, a tiny note.

'I am a Nazi,' it said. 'I was sent here to try to find out things about the Germans and Austrians who had been at your School. Now I have heard that my mother has disappeared, and I am going back to Germany to find out what has happened. I haven't done the School any real harm. I could find out so little at first, and later on I didn't try to. You've all been so good to me, I could not. Please forgive me, and oh, pray—for you believe in God and prayer, but I was taught that neither is any use—that my mother may be safe. I am sorry—I am sorry! Gertrud Becker. I have signed my proper name.'

To say that the School got a shock is scarcely adequate. Only Robin, Lorenz, and Polly were not surprised. The rest went round in a perpetual state of, 'I *say*!'

As for Miss Annersley, she told her colleagues that she could have beaten herself. 'Polly Heriot came and told me what she and Robin Humphries suspected,' she wailed, 'but I thought it was the usual spy-fever we always get in wars. The girl came to us with good credentials. I didn't laugh at Polly openly. One doesn't want to "daunton" young people, as the Scots say. But I didn't bother about it. And then Mademoiselle's death occurring at the same time put it right out of my head. And now—*this* has happened! Oh, where is that poor, plucky, silly child?'

CHAPTER XVIII

ADRIFT!

COULD Miss Annersley have seen the answer to her question, she would almost certainly have been even more horrified than she was. Gertrude or, to give her her proper name, Gertrud Becker was crouched in a tiny dinghy, in company with a Guernsey fisherman, looking with scared eyes at waves that seemed to her to be mountains high, though actually they were nothing out of the ordinary. There was a full tide running and what sailors call a good following wind from the west. But to Gertrude's inexperienced mind, it was a storm. She felt deathly sick, and only wished that she had stayed where she was. Then her thoughts turned to her mother, and she knew that she could have done nothing else, no matter how much she suffered.

They rowed on in silence. The fisherman had been well paid for his trouble, and all he had to do was to put this girl aboard a barque named the *Belle Marie*. Once that was done, his work was ended, and he could go home. As for Gertrude, her troubles would only just have begun.

On and on, up one monster green hillock, only to slide down the further side, and mount another. It seemed never-ending to the poor child in the stern of the boat. She lay limply, covered by a tarpaulin the man had, with rough kindliness, thrown over her, and wished that she could die. But at long length the never-ending journey finished. The boat reached the side of another vessel; there were loud hails, and after a brief colloquy, she was heaved up in the rower's arms, and passed on deck to another man, who handed her to a third. Then she was taken into a place the smell of which was indescribable, and put down somewhere. She felt the rough hairiness of coarse blankets against her face, and then she must have fainted. She roused up with the sting of raw brandy burning her throat and tongue, and found herself looking at a bare plank ceiling, very close to her, while the place was lit up by a dim blue light. She had gone to bed in her clothes, it seemed, though she found out afterwards that someone had removed her shoes, cap, and big coat. She was muffled in blankets, and she was warm. The heaving was not quite so bad in this much larger boat, and she felt as long as she lay still, she could keep the sickness at bay.

A big burly man suddenly rose from a locker where he had been sitting thoughtfully chewing a cud of tobacco, and came and bent over her, asking her in some sort of French how she felt now, and if she would like anything to eat.

The bare thought of food made Gertrude feel sick again, and she gasped out a hasty, 'Non, merci!' whereat he nodded, and returned to his seat. She had a tongue in her head, and if she wanted anything, she could ask for it. It was a mercy for her that Gertrude had fallen into kindly if rough hands. The *Belle Marie* was a French barque, doing, in normal times, a coasting trade in timber with Norway. Now she was sailing for Denmark for dairy produce. The master had been asked if he would take this girl and land her at Jelling on the Velle River, whither he was bound. A passport, carefully forged, though he did not know that, had been handed over with her, and her other papers were in order. He was told that her mother was dying, and she must get to Denmark as quickly as possible. He had agreed, and poor Gertrude was on her way back to the land of bondage.

It might have been worse, though Gertrude thought that impossible. After the good food to which the Chalet

School had accustomed her, the fish stews and strongly seasoned soups, which were what the men lived on principally, were horrible to her. She recovered from her seasickness on the third day, and even managed to get on deck for a few hours, where the strong sweet air of the open sea completed the cure. But she had no place to go to at night but that cabin with its awful mixture of smells, and she always felt sick when she returned to it.

On the fifth day out, when she came up on deck, she noticed that the men seemed uneasy. The look-out in the bows of the ship, and the other man in the crow's nest, as the little platform up the mainmast is called, were watching the horizon keenly. The boats were all in readiness to be lowered at a moment's notice, and the master of the barque led her up to one, and told her to stay beside it. His gestures were eloquent enough, if his language was Greek to her.

'Pourquoi?' she asked.

The answer she got was so much gibberish to her, except for one significant sound. She knew what "U" meant. So there were U-boats about! And when the war first broke out, she, in common with most other young Nazis, had rejoiced over the exploits of the U-boats! Supposing one torpedoed the barque! Supposing she were drowned! For the first time Gertrude realised what the U-boat campaign really means. She knew now what the people in the *Athenia* must have felt when, without a warning, there came the awful blow which forced them into little ship's boats, and out to the open sea, with the possibility of death by drowning or exposure before them. And she had rejoiced in the loss of the great liner! If ever a girl learned her lesson by bitter experience, Gertrud Becker was that girl.

They passed the coast of Holland, keeping well out beyond the three-mile limit. They were now coming up with the Danish coast, and then this nightmare of a journey would be over. Gertrude was thankful to know it. Soon she would be in Heidelberg now, and surely there would be some news of her mother.

She rejoiced too soon. Almost as she was thinking

142

this, obediently squatting beneath the ship's boat to which she had been assigned, the sound of a peculiar hissing and whinnying struck on her ear. Almost at the same moment there was a tremendous crash, and the bows of the *Belle Marie* were lifted clean off the sea, only to come down with a minor crash. There was no time to launch the boats. Almost immediately the *Belle Marie* began to settle down at the bows, and the captain, cursing the brutes who had done this thing to his beautiful ship, called a sharp word of command to one of the men, who advanced on Gertrude, picked her up, swinging her across his shoulders, and leaped with her into the sea with as long a leap as he could. With one hand, and his legs, he swam away from the ill-fated vessel with all his strength, for if they were caught in the swirl as she went down, nothing could save them. Gertrude had learnt swimming, and she had the sense to hold on to the man's shoulders, once she had recovered from the sudden shock of the icy water, so that his movements were as free as possible.

For some minutes he swam; then, with one arm supporting the child, he turned on his back, and looked towards where the *Belle Marie* had been. Nothing was to be seen of her but some wreckage; but near the same place there rose a great, whale-like shape, with water streaming from her sides, as she moved leisurely to the spot where her victim had been. Gertrude could see black, seal-like heads moving in the waters, and guessed that these must be some of the men. She was nearly frozen, but she managed to say nothing. Suddenly, as she watched, one of the three men who had come from the conning-tower and were standing on the streaming top of the submarine, glanced round behind where the girl and her rescuer were. What he saw there sent him down into the bowels of the vessel again with a sharp word to his two companions, who followed him at top speed. The conning-tower lid closed down with a clang, and the submarine submerged.

Gertrude's companion saw it as well. 'Vaisseau,' he said, as he turned once more and began swimming with her. Then he added, 'Anglais,' which seemed to be the limit of his French. Gertrude essayed a stroke or two, but she found her clothes, heavy with water, hampering, and, besides, she was stiffening with the chill of those chill seas.

But the British vessel had seen what had happened, and already boats were pulling away to pick up the survivors of the tragedy. It was barely a half-hour from the time of the torpedo explosion before they were safe again, among men who spoke English, though not the English to which Gertrude was accustomed. Then she saw a fair-haired boy of about eighteen, who was issuing orders, and at once the boat turned back to her mother-ship.

'We've got to get back,' announced the youthful commander. 'She's going to lay an egg or so and get that Jerry.—Oh, hang! I'll bet not a soul of 'em knows English! Wonder what their lingo is?'

'Breton, I think,' gasped Gertrude, who was rapidly succumbing to seasickness again. 'They know next to no French, anyhow.'

The boy glanced in her direction. 'Cripes! A girl!' he ejaculated.

Then he said no more, but bent his energies to bringing his boat alongside the destroyer without any mishap. She slipped into place, and five minutes later, Gertrude was helped out onto the deck by a tall, grave-faced lieutenant, whose reaction to her appearance seemed to be much what the boy's had been, judging by his expression when he saw her.

'A kid!' he exclaimed. 'You poor kid! Here! Come to my cabin at once. One of you chaps fetch the M.O. along as fast as you can.—Dicky, you carry on, my lad.'

Gertrude reeled, and collapsed into strong arms hastily extended to catch her. Once more darkness descended on her, and when she came to again, she was once more in a berth, but there was a difference. The cabin was sweet and fresh, and though painfully bare, everything was clean. A curtain hung over what she concluded was a doorway and they were proceeding with a long, steady rush that somehow seemed nearly smooth. She turned over. She felt stiff and bruised, and, as she suddenly realised, painfully empty.

Even as she thought of it, the door opened, the curtain was drawn back, and an elderly man, grey of head and clean-shaven of face, entered. As he met her eyes, his own brightened, and he turned and gave an order in an undertone before he came into the cabin and bent over her. 'Well, you look a little more alive,' he said in a deep, pleasant voice. 'Hungry, eh? Well,' as the door opened again, 'here's something to fill up the corners a bit.'

Sitting up, propped up with pillows, and attacking a bowl of soup which differed as much from the soup of the barque as chalk from cheese, Gertrude made up her mind on a certain point. She finished her meal, however, before she spoke. Then, when the man had taken the bowl from her, she looked at him rather piteously. 'I must see your captain. He won't want me aboard his ship when he hears, but I must tell him.' The man stretched out a hand, and felt her head. 'Cool,' he remarked *sotto voce*. 'What's worrying you, kiddy?'

'You see,' said Gertrude, stumbling a little, 'I'm not English. I'm a German—I *was* a Nazi. You can't want me here when you know that.'

The man grinned cheerfully. 'We don't war with women and kids,' he told her. 'As for Nazi, you say "were"?'

'I'm not now—I couldn't be. Not after they torpedoed us like that. Besides, the School made a difference. But I must see your captain and tell him.'

'Right you are,' said the man. 'You can have a bath and get your kit on. They've done the best they could with it, but I'm afraid it's seen its best days.'

He touched a button, and almost immediately a big sailor appeared bearing two steaming cans. He set them down, produced from the wall, with something of the air of one doing a conjuring trick, a big, round tin bath of the flat variety, which he set down. A huge sponge, flesh-brush, loofah, and soap were set out beside it, and

145

some hot towels. Then the two men retired, and Gertrude got up and made the best she could of her toilet. It was a bad best, she knew. Her serge skirt had shrunk, and her blouse would never be the same again. But at least the clothes were fresh and clean. There were brushes and a comb, and she contrived to reduce her hair to something like order. Then, donning her stained and shrunk coat, she opened the door, and ventured out into the grey-steel passageway with its lighting of blue bulbs. As if she had given a signal, the elderly man appeared from the door-way of another cabin, and she was taken to another cabin, where she told her whole story to a big man whose hook nose and black eyebrows meeting above his nose filled her with fear. However, she got through to the end, and then waited to hear the words that would turn her off this haven.

Instead, what happened was that the man stretched out his hand. 'Shake,' he said tersely. 'I like pluck.'

And that was all. Later, she learned that a radio message had been sent to Guernsey, thus relieving the hearts of a good many people, and then she was told that, as she had been put in the charge of the Chalet School folk, she was to be returned to them as soon as possible. Meanwhile, they were making for Scapa Flow, where she would be interviewed by the authorities.

'What—what happened to the submarine?' she asked shyly.

The captain's face became grim as he answered, 'We put paid to her account.'

'And the men from the barque? Did you save them all?'

'No,' he told her, still in that curt way.

'Oh, I'm so sorry!' Gertrude's eyes filled with tears. 'They were good to me in their way.'

'Fortune of war—fortune of the sea,' said the captain.

Then he turned her loose within certain bounds, and after a peaceful journey, and a few days spent in the great island-locked harbour of Scapa Flow, Gertrude was returned to the Chalet School, a wiser girl, a nicer girl, to find awaiting her a letter from her mother, stating that she was leaving for Denmark, and would write to her from there. Also, there was the biggest surprise the Chalet School had ever known in the whole of its career.

CHAPTER XIX

JOEY CREATES A SENSATION

DR CHESTER came down the stairs at Les Rosiers, grinning broadly. Joey had certainly done her best to provide the School and all concerned with a sensation this time, and he judged that she would have succeeded. He drew on his driving gloves, went to his car, and got in to drive to Bonne Maison to inform the young lady's sister of her latest exploit, in accordance with a promise young Mrs Maynard had got from him.

'Do go yourself, Peter,' she had implored. 'Don't just ring up or send a message. I'm dying to hear what Madge says and how she looks. You go; and tell me the whole story next time you come.'

'I'll go if you'll go to sleep without any more fuss,' he had said.

'Sleep? You couldn't keep me awake if you paid me for it!' retorted Joey, snuggling down among her pillows, and closing her eyes.

Two minutes later she was sleeping like a baby, and Nurse exchanged smiles with the doctor. 'What a patient! She won't be on our hands long at this rate! You'd better go and keep your word, Dr Chester.'

'All right. But don't let her talk much when she wakes up. Keep her quiet, and she'll be worrying the life out of all of us in three weeks' time by her monkey tricks.' With which speech he had departed.

He drove through the quiet country lanes, now strewn with leaves, pondering on what Mrs Russell would have to say. She herself was confined to the house with a bad bilious attack, following on the anxiety felt over Gertrud Becker's disappearance. Late the night before the radiogram had come, bringing news of that young renegade's safety and whereabouts, so that worry was at an end. And this other trouble which she had dreaded was practically over, too. But what she would say when she heard the news—! The doctor chuckled aloud as he swung his car in at the gateway of Bonne Maison, and drove up the short drive to the door.

Madge Russell was up today, and sitting in her room, Baby Josette slumbering placidly in her crib in the far corner. She was playing with some knitting, but she was rather bored by it, as well as anxious over her sister, whom she had not been able to see since her own illness. At sight of the doctor, therefore, she tossed her work down, and gave a welcoming cry.

'Peter Chester! Is Anne with you? This surely isn't a professional visit? I'm practically all right now. It was only a bilious attack. My tummy always goes back on me when I have any extra worry.'

The doctor sat down. 'Let's see your tongue? Now your pulse—may as well go through all the proper motions. Oh, you're all right!'

'Do you know how Joey is today?' asked Madge, leaning back in her chair.

'Simply splendid. You know, Madge, you're worrying yourself most unnecessarily about her. There's nothing wrong with Jo.'

'I've been mother to her so long,' said Madge. 'And for so long her health was such an anxiety to me.'

'Well, there's nothing to be anxious about now. She's as strong as a moorland pony.'

'Jem tells me the same thing. I'm glad to hear you agree. But I do worry over her.'

'No need to think of it.'

'I can't help worrying,' said Madge defensively.

'Well, don't. The time for worry is over!'

'What?' gasped Madge, suddenly galvanised into an erect position. 'Do you mean—it's happened?'

'Over,' his eyes wandered to the pretty old cuckoo clock on the wall, 'just three and a half hours ago.'

'Impossible!' Madge fell back in her chair, deprived of breath.

'Not at all.'

'Why wasn't I told?'

'Joey wouldn't have you worried. There wasn't any need. She's quite cheery, and fell asleep before I came along like a baby herself. She'll be up and about in three weeks' time. I can promise you *that*.'

Madge recovered herself. She sat up again. 'It's really all over? And well over, too. Oh, thank God!'

'She's extremely thrilled with life,' said the doctor pensively.

'And—which is it?'

He possessed himself of her wrist again. 'Let's be sure your heart's in good working order first. I must break this to you carefully. It's—prepare yourself for a shock! —daughters—three of 'em!'

'Three daughters! *Triplets!*' Madge was robbed of speech again. 'Peter! You aren't trying to pull my leg, are you?'

'Of course not! It really is three daughters. Jo calls them Jane, Joan, and Jean; but whether those will remain their names or not, I can't tell you.'

'Let's hope not! Where's Jem? Does her know? And Jack, with his regiment in France—have you wired him?'

'Wired him ages ago. As for your husband, so far as I know, he's at the San. No; he doesn't know yet. I'm leaving you to tell him.'

'Doesn't know what yet?' demanded Jem Russell's voice at the door. 'What are you yarning about now, Peter?'

'Oh, Jem! Joey's got triplets—girls! Isn't it just like her?'

Jem came into the room and sat down on the foot of the bed. 'Oh no, you don't, my dear!' he said jeeringly. 'I'm not going to fall for a tale of that kind, so don't you think it.'

'It's true! Ask Peter! He's just come from there.'

Jem turned to the other man incredulously. 'Is it really true?'

'Oh, quite. Jo made me promise to come and tell Madge, and I've to report, when next I see her, on the reaction. I should think even she will be satisfied. And,' he went on, getting up, and buttoning up his top-coat which he had opened on coming into the warm room, 'I am going to inform Anne, Janie, and Elizabeth now. I'll leave the School and the kids to you two.'

'And Dick,' said Madge excitedly. 'Jem, you must cable Dick and Mollie at once. Oh, won't they be thrilled?'

'Write your cable, and I'll send it off. I'm passing the post-office,' said the doctor.

'Right you are,' said Jem. 'Got any paper up here, Madge?'

'Yes; in that case over there. Oh, I simply must go and see Joey! Jem, will you run me round now if I wrap up?'

Her husband turned from the case where he was rummaging for paper. 'No fear! You've been in bed three days, and this is your first day up. You'll stay where you are for today. If you're all right, you can go tomorrow. But you'll wait till then. You don't want a chill on top of everything else, do you? Besides,' he added, 'if you went, it would probably excite Jo, as she knows how bad you've been, and that wouldn't be good for her. Just calm yourself, my dear, and make up your mind to stay where you are.'

His last argument settled the question. Madge was not going to do anything to upset Jo, and she knew how easily her sister was excited.

She sank back in her chair with a grimace. 'What a bully you are, Jem! All right; I'll wait till tomorrow. But mind, you've got to ring up Les Rosiers for the latest news. By the way, what about the children? They don't know, you say, Peter? But they mustn't come home! They'd much better stay at School. What time is it?'

'Half-past three,' said her husband, with a glance at his watch.

'Just nice time. I'll ring up Hilda and tell her the news, and ask if she can keep Robin and Daisy for the next day or two. The house ought to be kept quiet. Besides, there's only Anna there, and her hands will be full with the housekeeping.'

'Yes; I hadn't thought of that,' agreed Peter Chester.

'If it had been only Robin,' went on Madge, crossing the room to the telephone, 'it wouldn't have mattered. But Daisy's another pair of shoes altogether. Rob's quiet and gentle, but Daisy is a little tomboy, and she can't help making a noise. I'll tell Hilda that if they don't want to stay at School they can come here. They can sleep in that little room off the night-nursery, and we can move Rosa's bed into the night-nursery. It'll be only for a few days, won't it, Peter?'

'Oh, a week. But that's all,' agreed Dr Chester, as he waited for the cable. 'This the message, Jem? What a sensation it will create in India!' And he grinned as he read it.

'What have you said? Let me see!' Madge dropped the receiver, and craned her neck over her husband's arm to see.

' "Triplets at Les Rosiers. All shes." *Jem Russell!* They'll think it's some Nazi code message at the post-office!'

'I'll explain,' said Peter, chuckling. 'After all, it's the first time I've met with triplets in all my medical career. It'll create a sensation not only among ourselves and the School, but in the Island. Right you are, Jem. I'll send this off at once.'

He went off, followed by Jem, and Madge, after a glance at her own small daughter to be sure that she was still asleep, rang up the School and promptly became embroiled in an endeavour to persuade Miss Annersley that it was no joke, but that Joey really had accomplished the fact. But when she had taken it in, the Head laughed heartily.

151

'How like Joey! She always did do things in a whole-sale manner!'

'She did,' agreed the young lady's sister pensively. 'Any further news from Scapa, by the way?'

'My dear girl! Is it likely? I suppose the next thing will be that that poor child will be returned to us. I've kept it from the School, Madge. I've only let them know that Gertrude heard that her mother had disappeared, and she'd gone to Denmark to try to find her. All quite true, mercifully. What's that? Will I keep Robin and Daisy for a few days? Of course I will. They can't very well go home with Jack in France, and only Anna at the head of affairs. When are you going to see Jo?'

'Jem says if it's all right he'll run me over tomorrow, I'm longing to see her—and her triplets. You know, I simply can't believe it! It doesn't seem possible. Why, it's only the other day Jo was getting into the wildest mischief, and now she's a proud mamma!'

'The School will be excited,' said Miss Annersley. 'Do you know what she's going to call them?'

'Peter Chester *says* they're to be Jane, Joan, and Jean, but I hope not. I'm very tired of Joan for a name. Besides, we want a change from these interminable J names of ours.'

Then she rang off, and returned to her chair and to Baby Josette, who had wakened up and was complaining loudly that she wanted her tea. Madge got the hot milk and rusks, and fed her, and then had her own tea, while the blue-eyed baby crooned to herself in the big basket at the side of her chair.

The next afternoon Jem fulfilled his promise, and took his wife, well bundled up, across to Le Forêt where, in the big front bedroom of Les Rosiers, Joey lay chuckling to herself at intervals at the thought of all the talk there would be, and her daughters slept in the huge old double cradle that Mrs Chester had sent her from Pierres Gris only that morning. When her sister appeared at the door, she turned her head with a wide grin that made her startlingly like the wicked schoolgirl of five or

152

six years before, and observed, 'Hello, Madge! Come to welcome your nieces?'

Madge bent down and kissed her. Then she stood back and inspected her carefully. 'You look as fit as a fiddle.'

'I feel it. A bit groggy still, of course. But Nurse says that'll soon pass off. What do you think of the Family?' And she nodded towards the cradle.

'Yes; I must see them.' Madge went over and knelt down. The next moment, she was sitting back on her heels, rocking with laughter.

'What's the joke?' demanded Joey suspiciously.

'They're all right. Quite normal, and as pretty as most new babies are.'

'Oh, they *are*! They're lovely babies. But oh, Joey, this *is* a judgment on you! Do you remember how you yelled when you first saw Sybil because she had red hair? And now, every one of your babies has even redder hair than she! It serves you right! '

Joey laughed. 'Yes; don't they make a contrast to Jack and me. He is the world's fairest man, and I'm a crow. And here we are, blessed with ginger-headed daughters! '

'Oh, not ginger! ' protested Madge. 'It's much too deep a red for that! Joey, they *are* darlings! What are you going to call them?'

'Jane, Joan, and Jean.'

'Joey! You're *not*! '

'All right! Don't believe me if you don't want to.'

At this point Nurse intervened, saying that Mrs Maynard should rest now, so Madge had to go, with the question of the babie's real names still not settled, for she felt fairly sure that the names Joey had given her were not the real ones.

The next day a letter came from Jack Maynard, 'somewhere in France,' full of excitement about his newly arrived daughters, and asking for further details. *He* called them 'Maria, Eliza, and Martha'!

'Neither of them will give us a sensible answer! ' wailed Madge, who had spent an hour with her sister that morning, and found Joey even more blandly irritating than

153

before. 'What *can* they be going to call the poor babes?'

'Perhaps it's something so outrageous neither of them likes to tell us,' suggested Jem. He began to laugh.

'What are you laughing at?' demanded his wife.

'I was just thinking of the names party I held when Sybil arrived. It was just before half-term, you may remember, and a whole crowd of the girls were up at Die Rosen. I asked them each to choose one name, and the variety was—queer. Joey plumped for "Malvina." Do you think she can possibly be going to wish that on to one of those helpless infants of hers?'

'Not very likely. But I wish she'd talk sense about it,' said Madge crossly. 'Here are those babies, three days old, and no one—unless Joey and Jack do, which I doubt from the way they are going on!—has the faintest idea what they are to be called!'

'Jo calls them "One, Two, and Three" when there's anyone round,' observed Peter Chester, who was with them. 'It has a rummy sound. "Give me Three, Nurse, and you can put Two back into the cradle." '

'I might have known Jo wouldn't be sensible, even over her children,' said Madge, giving it up with a giggle at this information. 'Well, we'll just have to await her ladyship's pleasure, I suppose.'

That day word came from Scapa Flow that Gertrude was returning to the Chalet School as soon as she could be put across the Channel.

Two days later, when Madge was sitting by the fire holding the three babies on her knee, Jo, who was now propped up with pillows, and looking remarkably well, said casually, 'By the way, the babes are to be baptised the day after tomorrow.'

'Joey! Who are the god-parents, then?'

'Bill and Charlie and Nally. Sorry I can't have you, my dear, but as they'll be brought up Catholics, it can't be done.'

'I knew that, and didn't expect it. How are you going to get Grace Nalder across, though?'

'I can't. Rob's going to deputise for her. And Gottfried

Mensch, Eugen von Wertheimer, and Vater Bär will be godfathers.'

Madge rose, and laid the babies in the cradle. 'Jo,' she said, coming to kneel down by the bedside, 'tell me truly, what *are* their names to be?'

Mischief glimmered in Jo's black eyes. Then she relented. 'Right-ho! I'll tell you. One is to be Helena after Nell Wilson; Two is to be Constance, after Con Stewart; Three is to be Margaret after you. And they've all got Mary for a first name. Will that do?'

Madge drew a deep breath of relief. 'I've been wondering all sorts of things. You are so mad sometimes, Joey. But what are you going to call little Margaret? Not the whole thing, surely?'

'No, my dear. She'll be Margot to please Daisy.'

'Joey! What a dear thing to think of! Daisy will be so pleased!'

'I know, poor kiddy. And Helena is to be Len, and Constance will be Connie. I did try to think up three names all beginning with the same letter, but I couldn't get anything I wanted. I'd have liked to call one "Clare," but I couldn't think of a single other decent name beginning with C, so I gave it up.'

'Len, Connie, and Margot. They are pretty names, and thank goodness, you've gone off the J complex we seem to have had. You are Jo, and we've Jem and Jack, in the family, not to mention Jacky Bettany, and my own Josette. It's quite a relief to have other letters.'

'Well, your other two are David and Sybil. It isn't as bad as you make it sound. Now tell me what news there is of that poor child, Gertrude. When is she coming back?'

'Very shortly, I gather.'

'Good! I must try to be around to help to welcome her. Peter says I can be up to lie on the couch on the baptismal day. I'll soon be on my feet again. I never had the smallest use for lying in bed—except when the rising-bell at school went. I'll admit it was a bit of a strain at times to get up then.'

'Well, don't try to overdo. That's all I ask.'

'Give me credit for a little common sense! There's One—I mean Len—crying. Give her to me, Madge.'

Madge laughed as she got up to bring the baby. 'Joey, you're incorrigible!' she said.

CHAPTER XX

A STILL BIGGER THRILL

'AND now,' said Miss Wilson hopefully, 'perhaps we can settle down to ordinary school work for a change.'

'Perhaps—and perhaps not,' replied Miss Stewart pessimistically.

'Oh, don't be so gloomy! After all, except for Gertrude's little episode, it hasn't been such a bad term. You can't count Jo's slight effort as a *School* event.'

'*We* may not, but the *School* certainly does!' said Miss Annersley, laughing. 'I overheard Daisy Venables and Beth Chester talking under the study window yesterday. Beth was saying something about her twin brothers. "I don't think *twins* are anything much," says Daisy. "*We* have *triplets*! That's much more uncommon. Your own father says so!" Beth's face of fury—I peeped out behind the curtains—was a perfect treat.'

'Well,' Miss Stewart picked up a box, and made her way to the door of the Staff common-room, 'I must go. I'm due to teach my little angels how to bandage burns and scalds tonight.'

'And I must go to explain the inwardness of splints to the Seniors,' chimed in Miss Wilson. She turned to Miss Phipps, the Kindergarten mistress. 'May, how are you amusing your lambs?'

'With knots for bandages,' said Miss Phipps placidly. 'Also, the right method of using safety-pins. Peggy Burnett thinks that if you catch two edges together it's quite all right. And the last time Marie Varick pinned her bandages, she stuck the pin well into Marjorie Burn. You should have heard the yells!'

The three departed, and Miss Annersley and Mademoiselle Lachenais looked at each other and smiled. 'For these and all other mercies—' quoted Miss Annersley. 'Con seems very down today, Jeanne? Do you know what's gone wrong?'

'The mail has not come from Singapore,' said Mademoiselle. 'I think she is afraid that raiders or U-boats may be responsible.'

'Poor Con! In one way, though we shall miss her terribly, I shall not be sorry when her Jock makes the arrangements for the wedding.'

'It is not likely to be soon now,' returned Mademoiselle briefly.

'No; she cannot go there, and I doubt if he can get here. Oh, *drat* Hitler and all his works!' With which highly reprehensible remark the Head picked up her essay books and departed to the study, while Mademoiselle settled down to correct the Fourth's exercises, and to groan over Myfanwy Davies' ideas of French construction.

While the three first-aid enthusiasts were busy with the girls Miss Wilson had a fairly easy time, for most of this work was revision for the Seniors, who had done it in their Guide tests. But Miss Stewart found her own flock uncommonly stupid over the treatment of burns and scalds. As she was worried over the non-arrival of the mail, they found her far from pleasant, and she almost reduced Biddy O'Ryan to tears by her strictures on that young lady's attempts at bandaging a scalded foot. As Biddy had omitted to use any gauze or packing, this was scarcely to be wondered at. Still 'Charlie' was unduly sarcastic about it, and Biddy, as she unwound the careful figure-of-eight bandage with which she had swathed Inga Eriksen's foot, reflected sadly that there were times when you never could do right, no matter how hard you might try.

At last the hour was over, and the gong sounded for supper. Biddy thankfully rolled up her bandage, and put it away in the first-aid box with the others. Then she went to the dining-room, where they sat down to shepherd's-pie, followed by bread and butter.

After supper, there came an interlude for games or dancing in Hall until eight, when the Middles went to bed. The Juniors had gone before. The Seniors had till nine, when bedtime came for them.

The next day Joey appeared unexpectedly, bringing her babies with her. She declared that she had come to introduce them to their future School, and *not* to show them off, of which vanity she was accused by Cornelia Flower.

'Rubbish!' said Cornelia. 'You know well enough, Joey, that you're as proud as a cat with two tails at having trips.'

'At having *what*?' demanded Joey.

'Trips, honey—short for triplets. Just think! Madame's been married for nearly nine years, and she still has only three. And here are you, married well under two years, with three to match her. I guess she feels green sometimes.'

'That's nothing to what Marie von Wertheimer said when she first saw me,' said Jo, chuckling. 'She sounded as if I had insulted her personally by beating her like this.' She touched little Connie's head with one finger. 'They're rather nice, aren't they, Corney?'

'They're perfect ducks.' Then Cornelia lifted her enormous blue eyes to Jo's face. 'Joey! Have they heard anything of Dr von Ahlen?'

Joey shook her head, a shadow falling over her face. 'Not a word. I heard from Frieda last week—she wrote to congratulate me on being the mother of three—and she said that no one knew anything about him.'

'Poor Frieda! Oh, Joey! What a wicked thing all this is! And Gertrude hasn't heard another word about her mother since she came back. She's so afraid that something may have happened.'

'It's soon yet. Getting letters through, even from neutral

158

countries, is a bit of a job these days. I heard from Jack on Saturday, and not a line since!' The shadow deepened on Jo's face. 'It's a bit stiff.'

'He's all right, though,' said Cornelia. 'If he hadn't been, you'd have heard. Is there news of anyone else?'

'Bette and the children have reached Canada. My sister had a letter this morning. She's got a job as housekeeper to a farmer-man, out on the prairies. She's plucky, Corney. First she lost Giovanni; then she lost her home; and now she's lost every penny of her money, and has to start work. However, she's got little Giovanni and Marya, so she has something to live for.'

'Well,' said Cornelia sturdily, 'so have you—three little girls. I guess, whatever happens, you've got as much as most of us.'

'I guess I have.' Jo was silent for a few moments. Then she changed the conversation. 'What on earth have the Middles been doing with Charlie? Or rather, what has she been doing with them? I saw Biddy before I came along here, and she was full of some grievance to do with bandaging. Has Charlie been bandaging them and tying them up too tightly? Biddy was rather incoherent—and appallingly Irish—and the bell rang before I could make out what it was all about.'

'Oh, Biddy made a mull of her bandaging, and Charlie dropped on her rather heavily. I think that's about all. But Charlie is queer these days. Say, Joey! do you think she's scared of Singapore, and wants to back down, and doesn't like to say so?'

'Don't get mad ideas into your head, Corney!' Jo spoke with some sharpness. 'Whatever else it is, I'm perfectly certain it isn't *that*!'

Cornelia subsided, and devoted herself to the babies, who were, as their mother had proudly pointed out, 'growing wisibly.'

'I wonder,' said the younger girl pensively, as she sat nursing little Margot, 'what use all this first-aid will be to us? We aren't likely to have anything of that kind to do. If we *had* a raid and anyone got hurt, I guess Matey and Bill and Charlie would see to them. *We* shouldn't be trusted. So what's the use of learning it all, Joey?'

'You never know when *anything* may come in handy,' said Jo. 'Give me Margot, Corney! I must be getting home. They've been out quite long enough for a first time, even if it *is* nearly as hot as July today. I want to see the Abbess before I go, so I must fly.'

Cornelia handed over the baby, and grinned as Jo gathered the three up, rather as though they had been puppies. 'I wondered how on earth you managed to carry the lot at once. They're jolly good not to yell over it. Likely though,' she added, 'they're used to it by now.'

'What do you mean?' asked Jo indignantly. 'They're quite comfy. How d'you expect me to carry them? In my mouth by the scruffs of their necks? You haven't a lot of sense, even now, Corney!'

She marched out, leaving Cornelia chuckling over the touching picture her last words had called up, and went to seek Miss Annersley, who happened to be free, and who admired the triplets as much as heart could wish. Then she went home, where Robin and Daisy were waiting to see if they might help with baths, bottles, and bed.

The next day was Saturday, and as it was a fine, mild day, the Seniors begged permission to walk to Pleinmont, taking their tea with them. They could get a bus home about five, so the Head agreed.

'Don't try to paddle, though,' she warned them. 'For one thing, you know by now what the tides are like. For another, the day is warm enough; but it's more than the water will be. We are getting to the end of term, and I don't want any crop of colds to wind it up with. And mind you don't lose the bus, whatever you do.'

'We'll be careful,' promised Maria. 'And may we take Biddy and Nicole with us? The rest have lost their Saturday treat for mixing pepper with some of the chemicals in the chemmy lab. Those two were not in it, and they are rather dull.'

'Yes,' said Miss Annersley, 'if they will promise to do as you tell them.' She managed to keep a straight face as she spoke, but it was with difficulty, and she was thankful when Maria curtsied and withdrew, so that she could indulge in the wild laughter that possessed her. For the prank played by the Fourth on Miss Wilson had been one of the funniest things that had happened since the Chalet School had come into being again. Seven naughty Middles, at the instigation of Elizabeth Arnett, who had thought of it, had mixed pepper, and black pepper at that, with some chemical that, being more or less harmless, was left on the open shelves in its glass jar. It had been done when Mary Shand had been sent across by 'Bill' to bring some exercise books which had been left there by accident.

The result was that 'Bill,' needing the stuff—it was powdered charcoal—for some experiment with the Fourth, had tipped it out, and the resultant sneezing-match had been cataclysmal. The mistress, stooping over the compound, had got most of it, and had sneezed until the tears poured down her face, and she was speechless. Biddy O'Ryan and Nicole de Saumarez, who had known nothing about it, had been close enough to get a quite healthy minor dose. The rest, being in the know, had warily kept at a distance. This was a pity from their point of view. When 'Bill' reviewed the whole matter later on in her own mind, she had leapt to the conclusion that the pair affected had been innocent of the mischief, while the rest had all had a finger in the pie. Therefore, no treat for all of the Fourth, excepting Biddy and Nicole, who had been very indignant about the whole affair. Those two went off rejoicing with the Fifth and Sixth, while the rest sat in their form-room, laboriously stitching at the hems of sheets which Matron had selected as a suitable penalty for them.

The party who set out, were very much on their good behaviour. They were proud of being trusted like this, and, besides, they had the two Middles with them. Cornelia and Maria headed the little procession, and the rest tailed after them in twos, until they were beyond

161

houses, when they broke file, and drew together in groups of three or four.

'Where are we going?' asked Nicole, an Islander herself, but from Jersey.

'To Pleinmont—where the witches and Gens du Vendredi keep Witches' Sabbath every Friday night,' replied Cornelia with a wicked glance at Maria. It was well known that Nicole had her full share of Island faith in the unhallowed doings of the Gens du Vendredi, as suspected witches and wizards are called in Guernsey. She had had an old Guernsey nurse who had told her countless legends, and though she always *said* she didn't believe in them, it was only partly true.

At Cornelia's words, Nicole shivered, and drew nearer to Polly Heriot, the nearest Senior. Biddy O'Ryan, a wild Irish girl from Kerry, shivered too. You can't grow up on a mental diet of banshees and other Irish superstitions without being a little afraid of uncanny beings.

'Don't look so scared, you two!' said matter-of-fact Polly. 'Even if such things existed—and they *don't*—they couldn't hurt you today. This is Saturday, not Friday.'

Thus reassured, the pair looked a little ashamed of themselves, and trotted along with Inga Eriksen and Kitty Burnett of the Fifth, while the rest strolled on, discussing the netball and lacrosse teams with a point and fervour that was worthy of a better cause.

They reached the great sweep of Rocquaine Bay, where the Gens du Vendredi hold their Friday night dances, and settled themselves on one of the great concrete banks that run down from the road to the shore. The sun was shining, and they were in thick coats. They decided to have their tea at once, though lunch was barely two hours past, and then spend the rest of their time in climbing about.

Tea was as nice as it usually was, and they ate it as if they had had no food for a week. When they had finished, and all the scraps of paper had been tidied away into the baskets, Cornelia suggested that they should climb the sandy path up Pleinmont Point and see what the view was like today.

'It won't be up to much,' said Polly. 'There's a thin mist over the sea. Still, it's always fun to climb. I do miss the mountains.'

'Oh, so do I,' agreed Cornelia. Then she glanced at Maria, who was standing within earshot. The girls were very careful what they said in front of their Head Girl these days. There was still no news of Herr Marani, and it seemed almost certain that he was dead. Maria never spoke of it, but her young face had grown even graver during these past weeks, and she rarely talked much—Maria, who had been so gay and merry and chatty until all this had happened!

However, on this occasion she was laughing at Biddy, who was trying to turn head over heels, and failing ignominiously every time.

'Can't you do *that*?' demanded Cornelia. 'Here! Clear the fairway! *I'll* show you!' But she had the caution to glance round to see that no one was in sight before she began. Then she swung over, and turned a series of almost perfect cartwheels down the concrete slab, pursued by shouts of laughter and cries from the others.

'Corney! You might remember you're a prefect now!' scolded Violet when the acrobat came back up the slab, breathless and grinning. 'Suppose the Abbess or Bill had seen that exhibition!'

'It would have rejoiced Bill's heart,' said Cornelia calmly. 'She is nuts on keeping yourself fit—I say! What's that?'

The others stopped their chatter to listen to the sound that had caught her sharp ears. Far away, very faintly through the wreaths of mist it came—the sound of an aeroplane engine, throbbing with a broken note like a wounded thing.

Like most of their generation, the girls knew enough about aeroplanes to realise that this one was in difficulties. Eagerly they stared across the grey, heaving sea, but they could see nothing.

'Run, Polly, and see if you can get help from someone!' cried Maria. 'She's in difficulties, and she may crash.' She looked round the band. 'Robin, you scoot, too, and ring up the fire-station. She may burn if she crashes. You two kids get up the road, and behind that cottage. I'm responsible for you, and I'm not going to have you hurt if I can help it. Knock at the door and tell them. They may be able to help, too.'

'They can't! It's La Rochelle, the Lucys' summer house, and there's no one there now!' cried Robin from the road which she had gained. 'And it's no use going to that next one, either, because there's only old Mrs de Garis there, and she's almost blind, and crippled, too! The nearest place is those fishermen's cottages down the road. The bungalows are always empty at this time of year. People only use them in the summer. The hotel may be open, though. I'll 'phone the San—at least I'll try it!' And she legged it down the road at top speed.

All the time, the throbbing, broken note was coming nearer and nearer, and presently they could see her through the mist—a small aeroplane, with shattered fuselage, and wings riddled with bullets. There was other trouble, too, for even as they watched, the note changed again, and the birdlike thing sank near the water. Then she struggled to rise again, to reach the shore. Up, up, she lifted herself, very slowly, moving by jerks till she was, perhaps, twenty feet above the surface. She was now so near, that they could clearly see the swastika that showed the plane to be German, and one man leaning helplessly against the side of the cockpit.

'She's going to crash!' cried Cornelia. And even as she said it, the great thing lifted with a sudden spasm, and then crashed headlong on to the sands, her under-carriage crushed to atoms; her great planes broken and battered; a thin stream of smoke beginning to pour from her tail. Almost at the same moment, a figure rose, and, seizing the helpless man in the cockpit, took a wild leap from its edge on to the sands. They fell, rolling over and over, and flames leaped heavenward from the damaged thing on the sand, while the two men lay there, helpless, inert, apparently dead.

With a wild cry, Cornelia sped down the runway to the beach, followed by Maria, Violet, Sigrid, and Yvette. The rest were waved back by Maria with a gasped, 'Go for help—quick! Bring doctors!' as she raced after the Games Captain, whose long legs brought her rapidly to the stricken pair.

But rescue was not easy. The men had fallen near the plane, and the heat of the flames was terrific. For a moment Cornelia drew back, and no one can blame her. Then she set her teeth. The Chalet School mustn't have a coward in it. She remembered how Hilary Burn had plunged into Hall after Jo's first book when Anne Seymour had set the place on fire with the electric iron; and this was a question of the life of one man, if not of two. With an inarticulate prayer for courage, Cornelia leapt on the first man, catching him by his shoulders, and dragging him away from the flames. He groaned as she moved him, which relieved her for the moment. Then she saw that Maria and Violet were tackling the second. Maria's long, thick hair had fallen down from the knot on her neck in which she had worn it since her eighteenth birthday, and it fell across her face. She could not take time to put it out of her eyes, and a shower of sparks fell on it. Cornelia dropped her man, who was now away from the flames, sprang forward once more, and crushed out the sparks with her bare hands. In the excitement she never felt the pain. Neither did Maria realise at the moment what was happening.

Meanwhile, the rest of the Fifth and Sixth had reached them, and while four of them picked up Cornelia's rescue, and lugged him further up the beach, the others helped with his mate. Only Lorenz, Amy, and Enid left the men, and, racing as near to the burning plane as possible, began to scoop up the sand with their hands, and fling it on the flames.

'We must try to put it out,' gasped Enid. 'There may be valuable photos or notes on it. It may have been doing reconnaissance work.'

By this time, a small crowd began to pour down

on to the beach, and while some people took charge of the men, others came to heap sand on the flames. Some of the men had brought spades, and at last the fire was deadened. Not before most of the plane had been burnt out, though. There came a violent hooting, and then a car drew up, and Dr Chester leapt out. It was followed by two more cars, containing Jem Russell and another of the doctors from the Sanatorium. They hurried over to where the two men lay, and knelt down beside them.

Presently, Jem came to the girls, where Maria was beginning to find out that her hands were badly scorched. Cornelia had lost her front hair, and most of her eyebrows and eyelashes, and her face was smarting, while her hands were throbbing so, that she could scarcely keep from crying with the pain. Violet was not much better. These three were the worse off; the others were slightly scorched and bruised, but, as Jem found out, no worse. Cornelia, Maria, and Violet were packed into one of the cars, and driven off to the Sanatorium, where the burns were attended to before they were tucked up in bed to recover from the shock. The others were also sent home, but by bus, since there was no one else in it, and Jem Russell tipped the man heavily to drive straight to the School, where they created a minor sensation by their arrival in state. Dr Chester, when he had helped with the men, and seen to their being handed over to the proper authorities, had gone to the Pleinmont Hotel, where, earlier on, Robin had succeeded in getting himself and the Sanatorium on the 'phone. The doctor rang up Miss Annersley, so beds were ready and waiting for the girls, and 'Matey' ordered them off and forbade anyone to speak to them till she gave leave.

Only, when Dr Chester was going the rounds at ten o'clock that night, Biddy O'Ryan, who was awake, clung to him with both hands.

'Doctor Chester,' she said solemnly, 'will yez believe it? After all our work with burns and scalds the other day, niver a wan of us got a chance to show that we knew it!'

166

'You don't say so?' returned the doctor with equal solemnity. 'Whoever would have thought it?'

CHAPTER XXI

CONSEQUENCES

JOEY had been a prisoner for three days, thanks to that mist which the Chalet School Seniors had watched when the aeroplane accident had happened. From being a thin veil, it had grown denser and denser till, as Janie Lucy complained over the telephone to her new friend, 'You couldn't see your own nose, let alone your hand before your face.'

However, a brisk wind the night before had blown it away, though rags of it still lingered in the hollows. Therefore Jo, wrapping up her babies warmly, and disposing them comfortably in the big basket slung across the back seat of the car, decided that as the sun was shining and it was a mild day, she would make a tour. She wanted to go to the Sanatorium, where Maria, Cornelia, and Violet still were, though Violet, who had come off fairly lightly, was to return to School next day. The other two were likely to remain in their present quarters for some time yet. Cornelia's hands had been badly burned; and Maria, once it was all over, had collapsed with something very like a nervous breakdown. Small wonder, either. First there had been the wild flight from Austria. Then there had been the knowledge that she dared not return to her own country as long as the present régime remained in power—and Maria loved her country with a passion common to most Tyroleans. Then there had been the long-drawn agony of uncertainly about her father. Finally, came the accident, the burns, and the shock from which she was slow in recovering.

One bad trouble had been removed, though she did not know of it yet. Two days after the accident, a letter came from Frau Marani to Madge, saying that Herr Marani's ashes had been received by relatives of theirs. There was no explanation of how he had died; but at least the horrible uncertainty was over. His wife begged Madge to break the news to Maria, but the doctors had forbidden it until she was stronger. Then it would be a relief to her. At present, they thought she had as much as she could bear.

After visiting the invalids, Joey decided that she would go on to the School and see if there were any news of Gertrude's mother. Also, she must inquire why no one had been to see her these last few days. *She* was tied with the triplets; but surely *someone* from the School might have been over—more especially since both Robin and Daisy had been kept in the house by severe colds in the head. Joey had packed them both off to bed at the first signs, and kept them there in charge of Michelle, her nurse, while she herself looked after the babies. She had obediently kept away from them, for, as her brother-in-law had pointed out, she couldn't afford a 'flu' cold at present, with three infants on her hands. No one had seemed to bother about the pair, and she was badly puzzled by it. She had tried to ring up, but got no answer; or else she found the 'phone 'engaged.'

After the School, she thought she would run on into Peterport. The babies were running short of frocks, which was scarcely surprising, as no one had anticipated triplets, and she hadn't provided for them. She could get some in town, and then continue her journey as far as Les Arbres, the Lucys' home, where she proposed to spend the rest of the day.

'No need to ring up,' she decided. 'If Janie isn't at home, Nan will be. I'll take over the Christmas things for the babes, and that will be *one* job done, anyhow. Where's André, I wonder?' For Jem had forbidden her to drive the car at present, and had sent over his own man that very morning to see if she would like a run.

André turned up in the garage, and agreed to take her wherever she liked. The babies were dressed, and tucked up in their basket. They were good little things, spending most of their time in sleeping, and only crying on those occasions when, as their mother phrased it, 'Any self-respecting babe would yell.'

Then Joey got into her cap and coat and scarf, and looking with the pink in her cheeks more like a schoolgirl than ever, settled herself comfortably in the front seat beside André, and they drove off, going round by Torteval to give her a glimpse of Madge.

That lady was discovered in the midst of Christmas cooking. Joey dismissed André for half an hour, brought the babies in, and perched herself on the dresser to chat with her sister, while she watched the compounding of the Christmas cake.

'If it weren't for the children, I shouldn't bother at all,' sighed Madge, putting back a wisp of hair with a floury hand. 'But it *is* the children's festival, and one doesn't want to sadden it for them. Poor Onkel Florian! Who knows what he must have suffered in Germany!'

'Well, we may be thankful that it's over now,' said Joey gravely. 'Oh, how I would like to put Hitler, Göring, Goebbels, and the rest into the very worst concentration camp there is! And *then* their suffering couldn't pay for what they've done!'

Madge stirred her mixture carefully before replying. 'Isn't that rather against the feeling of the League, Joey?'

'*No!*' said Joey vehemently. 'I don't hate Germans— I'm too sorry for them, poor wretches! But those men aren't human! They're Evil made flesh, and we *must* hate what is Evil!'

Little Len uttered a cry just then, so Joey ceased her diatribe, and got down from her perch to hush her. Madge smiled as she watched them. 'They're lovely, Joey. And how they are growing! They'll be quite big girls when Jack sees them. Do you know when he gets leave?'

'This year—next year—some time—never,' quoted Joey. 'I've no idea. I wish he could get it. I'm dying to show him his daughters!'

'Well, it may come soon,' said Madge soothingly. 'Do

169

you mind coming away from that cupboard, Jo? I want a cake-tin or two.'

Joey moved from the cupboard-door against which she had been leaning.

'That's a sloppy way to cook! You ought to have got your tins ready first. Frau Mieders always taught us that.'

'I dare say! When you've got a baby to look after, and two small people to watch as well, you can't do everything according to Cocker!' retorted Madge. 'Where are those two, by the way? They're awfully quiet. Do go and see what they're after, Jo, while I get this into the tin!'

'Right; but leave me some decent scrapings if I do,' bargained Jo.

'Jo Maynard! You baby! Fancy wanting cake-scrapings at your age! And with a family of your own into the bargain!'

'I'll want cake-scrapings when I'm ninety and have great-great-grandchildren—always supposing I live as long,' returned Jo, departing to seek Jacky and Sybil, whom she found busy with scrap-books, and quite good and happy, if very sticky.

Then she called André, said goodbye to her sister, and went off in the car to the Sanatorium, where she speedily got leave to see the invalids, though Matron warned her that she must not excite Maria.

'She's in a highly nervous state, and it's only four days ago, Mrs Maynard. Don't stay long, and don't say anything likely in upset her.'

'I won't. I'm bringing the babes in, and we can talk about them. You can scarcely call triplets exciting as a topic of conversation.'

Matron laughed. 'I don't know about that. Your triplets have caused quite a lot of excitement in the place. They *are* doing well, though. How they are growing! And they're so bonny and firm,' she said.

Jo nodded, and went off, her basket in her arms, to seek Violet, as the strongest of the trio.

She found the librarian of the Chalet School busy

with a large jig-saw, from which she sprang up with a cry of welcome as Jo and her burden appeared in the doorway. 'Joey! And the triplets, too! How nice of you to come! Can you stay a while?'

'Half an hour or so. I want to see you all. And then I'm going over to School, and on into town.—What on earth is the matter with you, Vi?' For Violet had uttered an exclamation.

'You can't take the babies to School, Joey! You simply must *not*!'

'Why on earth not?' demanded Joey, excusably amazed at this.

'Don't you know? Hasn't anyone told you? No; I suppose they've all been too busy. They've got German measles, of all things! It's only the Juniors, so far; but you can't take three babies not six weeks old into German measles!'

'Good heavens! I should think not! But what about you and the others? Aren't you in quarantine, too?' Joey clasped her precious basket, and moved away to the door.

'Dr Jem doesn't think it's necessary. It began with Nancy Chester and Julie Lucy. Julie was first, and Mrs Lucy rang up at once to warn the Abbess. They closed the Junior school, of course. But the Second Form are boarders, all except Nita Eltringham. They *may* have caught it.'

'But—what about *our* kids? I've just come from my sister's, and she never said a word!' cried Joey.

'She wouldn't know. It only developed this morning. Dr Jem was in twenty minutes before you came, and said he was taking the children home, so he wasn't going to ring up,' explained Violet.

'Oh, what a mess! And I'd meant to go over to Les Arbres and spend the day there. Now, I suppose, I'd better trot home again, after I've seen you all. But I'll leave the babes with Matron, I think.—Oh! Rob and Daisy! What on earth am I to do with them?' And Jo stood stock-still, consternation growing in her eyes.

'Ring up the Abbess and ask her to keep them at School,' suggested Violet. 'Maria and Corney won't be going back for the rest of this term, so their beds will be vacant.'

'But what about you?'

'Oh, I've *had* it—years ago, when I was an infant of three or four. They say you never get it a second time, so I'm safe. And I'm really all right now. My face isn't sore now; and my hands have only one or two tiny places—nothing to worry over. Corney and Maria bore the brunt of it, I'm afraid. Corney's hands are very bad, Nurse told me.'

'Poor Corney! She's been a real heroine, from all accounts.'

'She was,' said Violet gravely. 'She got to that first man—the one who was nearest the plane, you know— and dragged him out of danger before even Maria and I had got round to thinking again. Did you know that the other man was dead even when the first jumped with him?'

Joey nodded. 'Jem told me. He'd been shot. Does anyone know the whole story yet?'

'No, and I don't suppose we out here ever shall. It was a German plane, though no one knows how it arrived here in that condition. The survivor is only just recovering from his concussion, and they can't ask him anything yet. But they must have had a bad time. What they saved of the plane was simply riddled with bullets, Nurse told me. Besides, we could see it for ourselves when she came down, before she took fire. It was a horrible business altogether.' And Violet shuddered at the memory.

Jo acted promptly. 'Sit over there in that chair, and I'll give you all three of the babies in your lap. Then you can say you were the first of the girls—after Rob and Daisy—to nurse them. There you are. Margot on the left; Len on the right; Connie—she's the quietest of the three—in your lap. Aren't they rather ducky?'

'They're lambs! Aren't they pretty? What very dark eyes Connie has, Joey! The other two have quite blue eyes; but hers look nearly black.'

'They probably will be presently,' said Jo calmly. 'As

172

for the other two, Margot's ought to remain blue all her life. Did you ever see anything so vivid in your life. I rather think, Len's may go grey or blue-grey when she's a little older.'

'Well, there's one thing,' said Violet, cuddling her burden, 'you'll always be able to tell them apart if their eyes are different.—There; go to Mummy, Margot!'

'Oh, I'm not going to be "Mummy" to them,' said Jo, comfortably assured that she was going to make a small sensation by her next statement.

'What, then? Small children find "Mother" awfully difficult to say. You surely aren't going all modern and letting them call you "Jo"?'

'No fear! Jack would have something to say about *that*. He has quite old-fashioned ideas in some ways, you know. No; they're going to call me "Mamma," and him "Papa." And Joey grinned as she saw Violet's jaw drop.

'"Mamma and Papa!" Joey! What on earth *for*? I thought no one ever did in these days.'

'Then I'll set the fashion.'

'Do you really mean it?'

'Oh, yes. I'm sick of "Mummy" and "Daddy," you see. And "Father" and "Mother" are, as you say, difficult for tinies. So I decided to come over all Victorian, and make "Mamma" and "Papa" of it. I talked it over with Jack ages ago, and he agreed with me. Now I must go to Corney. Give me my babies, and let me depart.'

'It's to be hoped they don't make "Momma and Poppa" out of it,' suggested Violet; whereat it was Joey's turn to look blank.

'It's to be hoped they *don't*! I'll sit on the faintest suggestion of that, I can tell you!—There you are, Margot, mein Vögelein; safe in your nice basket!' She tucked them in, and then, with a kiss blown in Violet's direction, took up the basket and backed out.

Cornelia was her next call after she had left the babies in Matron's charge, and she found that young lady lying in bed, looking curiously unlike the Corney of old, with all her lashes and brows gone, and a frizzled patch where short, fair curls used to tumble over her brow.

'Corney! You poor old girl! What a mess you look!' Was Jo's tactful greeting as she stooped over the invalid.

Cornelia's bandaged arms went up to hug her feebly, and Cornelia herself laughed. 'Oh. I know I look fierce! But it might have been worse. My eyes were so sore up till today, I was afraid they'd been really damaged. Dr Jem says it was only the heat of the flames. They're all right now; only I can't bear any strong light on them yet.'

Jo sat down on the side of the bed, and Cornelia shuffled over, and leaned against her. 'It's been rather—awful, wondering if they were really hurt. They were bandaged, you know, and I've had treatment for them. Dr Jem says I'll have to wear glasses for a while, until they are really strong again. But I don't mind that. Oh, Joey, I thought I was going to be blind!'

Joey hugged her gently. 'You poor old girl! I never thought of that. Thank goodness it'll be all right soon! And your hair and lashes and eyebrows will soon grow in again, Corney. You're not permanently disfigured.'

'Joey, d'you know what? I'm *glad* Mademoiselle didn't live to see it. She would have worried so. I never thought,' added Cornelia wonderingly, 'that I could say that; but I *can*. If it had happened while she was Head, she'd have been real upset. The Abbess has been in an awful stew about it, and she never had so much to do with me as Mademoiselle. She was here this morning. Say, Joey! D'you know they've got German measles?'

'Violet broke the glad news to me. You'd almost think the Gestapo had sent German measles after us on purpose! I'm going to ask the Abbess to take Rob and Daisy at School. If Rob gets it, I shall be torn in two. I'll be aching to nurse her; and yet I can't leave the babies, and they're much too tiny to risk German measles.'

'The Abbess says she doesn't think any of the Seniors will catch it. If Daisy stays, she'll be parked with the rest of the Middles. But it's mainly the babes, and we don't see so very much of them. Thinking of babes, where are yours?'

'Matron has them. I'm leaving them with her till I go. I was warned not to excite you, and above all not to excite Maria. So they're best where they are. Don't fret, Corney. You shall see them another day. Do you know how long you are likely to be here?'

Cornelia shook her head. 'I've not the least idea. Till my hands are better, anyhow. That's likely over Christmas.' She laughed forlornly. ''Tisn't my idea of a good Christmas—to spend it in San.'

'Oh, I expect you'll be able to leave before then,' said Jo. 'If so, you must come to me, Corney. I'll see you have a decent Christmas.'

'That's real good of you, Jo,' said Cornelia gratefully. 'But won't Dr Jack be with you for it?'

Jo shook her head. 'I don't know. I hope so, but I doubt it. He's said nothing in any of his letters.'

'Oh, Joey! It'll be hard lines if you can't spend your Christmas together! And the first after you've become Poppa and Momma—Say! What's biting you now?' For Jo had risen from the bed with some dignity, and was looking down at her haughtily.

'Only that you may as well understand that the children are not to be taught to call us anything of the sort. We are Papa and Mamma, and I'll thank you to keep to that!'

Cornelia chuckled feebly. 'Sorry! I didn't mean to get your goat. Do you really mean that, Joey? You do? Well,' after a pause, 'I can't say I'm surprised. You always did do things like no one else.'

After which, Jo took her leave, and went to make her last call. She found Maria in a darkened room, her hands and arms, like Cornelia's, bandaged; her face white, with great bruises under the eyes. But at the sound of Joey's voice, she lifted her long dark lashes, and looked up. 'Joey!' It was little more than a whisper, but Jo heard it.

'Maria, darling, I've come to see you. No; don't try to

talk. I'm not talking, anyhow. I'm just going to sing to you.'

Maria closed her eyes, and a faint smile crept to her lips. 'So nice,' she whispered.

Joey sat back in her chair, and singing pianissimo, but with every golden note as true as a nightingale's sang the old German carol, 'Silent Night, Holy Night.' Maria lay quietly, and under the cover of the bed-clothes, Joey could see that she was rigid. Occasionally, long tremors ran down her, and the elder girl felt frightened. Surely, even the long strain and the shock of the accident couldn't have had all that effect on Maria. Perhaps she wasn't fit for even singing yet. She ended the carol, and then half-rose to go. But Nurse signed to her to sit down again, and continue. Joey obeyed, and this time she sang the naïve children's carol, 'How far is it to Bethlehem?' She sang it with the utmost simplicity, and when she ended the last verse she saw that the awful rigidity was passing. Maria looked more natural, though she was still deathly white.

'One more,' said Joey gently, 'and then I must go.'

She paused, raking her mind for something that would be soothing and comforting. Suddenly she began, this time, the old 'Sleep, my Saviour, Sleep.' Her voice rose, sweet and full of tears, as she sang the pathetic carol. She was still for a moment when it ended. Then Nurse quietly pulled her out of the chair, and pushed her from the room.

'Have I done her any harm, Nurse?' asked Joey in a terrified whisper, for she had seen the silent tears rolling down Maria's cheeks as she passed the bed.

'No! You've done her all the good in the world. We couldn't break that awful calm of hers. The doctors were afraid of a bad illness for her if it continued much longer. Your singing has saved her that. She'll get better now. Now you go to Matron and get your babies, my dear. I must go back to her. But thank you from all of us for what you've done this afternoon!' To Jo's great surprise, Nurse, never a demonstrative person, reached up and kissed her before she vanished into the room,

176

leaving a thoughtful Joey to go along the corridors to Matron's room, where she retrieved her babies, and sent for André and the car.

She gave up her trip to the town, and bade André drive her home. She sat by his side, pondering on all the results of the accident.

'Vi made quite chatty! Corney stirred from her grief about Mademoiselle—for she *has* fretted badly—and able to feel glad that she's gone! And Maria—well, I expect they'll tell her about poor Onkel Florian now, and then she'll begin to get better, for she'll know that her mother will need her! And all that from an accident! Here we are, home again! Now if there's only a letter from Jack.'

Joey went slowly up to the house, bearing her basket. Then she entered, and it was as well for all concerned that Anna came into the hall to tell her of a telephone message which had come for her from the School. For as Anne left the kitchen, a tall, beloved figure appeared at the drawing-room door, and with a cry, Joey let go her burden, which was caught in the nick of time by the faithful maid, and flung herself, half-laughing, half-crying, into her husband's arms.

'Oh, Jack—Jack! Now I haven't a wish left unsatisfied!'

CHAPTER XXII

A FINAL SENSATION

'JACK, I'm going over to School this morning. Hilda rang me up to say that all fear for the Seniors and Middles is over. They break-up tomorrow, so I'd like to see them and show them you and the babies before they go. Are you coming with me?'

Jack Maynard looked up from his letters with a slight

177

grin. 'Oh, may as well. It's a glorious day. But you aren't going to make an exhibition of me, my dear, so get that out of your mind at once. I don't mind your exhibiting our daughters.'

Jo laughed. 'You're obviously almost fit, now. That's good! Oh, what a term this has been! In fact, what a two years—or almost—it has all been! Little did I think two years ago that I should be living in Guernsey, your wife, *and* Mamma to three!'

Jack rose, folding up one of his letters and slipping it into his pocket. The rest, he shuffled into a drawer. Jo watched him.

'Anything of interest?'

'Oh, so-so!' He carefully purged excitement from both voice and face, for he had had really thrilling news, but he had no intention of telling Jo yet, though he knew that when she heard it, she would be wildly excited. 'I've to go before the Medical Board next week. I expect they'll pass me as almost fit now. So make the most of me, young woman. They'll send me back to France once I'm passed.'

The laughter died out of Jo's face. 'I wish you hadn't to go. I do feel lonely when you're away. And the girls will grow up, and you will miss all the jolly part of their first teeth, and seeing and hearing them begin to walk and talk. How I do loathe this horrible war!'

'But if it is necessary, Joey? If it's to drive something utterly evil from the world?' He took her face between his hands, and looked down into the black eyes that were soft behind a film of tears.

Jo nodded. 'Yes; you must go. I see that. But I couldn't be quite resigned to it, and you don't expect it, either.'

'No; I don't expect it. But, Joey, remember that if you are lonely you might have been lonelier. You have the children. In the background are Madge and Robin and Jem, and the rest of the kids. Lots of women have had to say goodbye to their men with none of that to comfort them. And now,' he added in a different tone of voice, 'go and get yourself and the babes ready, and

I'll tell Batey to get the car out. With any luck, I'll be driving it myself next week.'

Jo smiled, and went off obediently. After the first wild joy of her husband's return had passed, there had been anxiety for her. Jack had come home on sick leave after a short, sharp attack of pleurisy. He had insisted that she must know nothing about it at the time. But when the first greetings were over, he had told her gently that he had three weeks' leave, and that he had been badly ill a month before. It had cast a shadow over her happiness, and she had been inclined to worry about him. However, in the soft air of Guernsey, and with home comforts round him, he had rapidly recovered, and was now almost in normal health again.

'I can't grouse,' she thought, as she rolled the babies in their shawls, and then tucked them into the basket they were beginning already to outgrow. 'Bless me! This thing isn't going to be useful much longer! What a size the children are getting!' She bent over the three tiny mortals, with their red heads all together on the pillow, gloating over their rosy cheeks. They were beautiful babies. They had been very small at first; but they were now progressing excellently, and were, as all the doctors assured her, three of the healthiest infants to be found in the Island. 'And I'm as fit as a fiddle,' she continued, as she pulled out her big coat from the wardrobe and slipped it on. 'I've a lot to be thankful for. But—I can't feel awfully thankful all the time.'

It was not until they had left the car at the lodge gates to the school in charge of Batey, who was Jack's batman, that the young doctor, carefully carrying the basket in which his daughters lay, making little inarticulate sounds, even mentioned his news.

'Joey,' he said then, calling his wife's attention from the healthy-looking borders entrusted to the care of the Middles, 'you've never asked me any more about my letters.'

Joey turned to him astonished. 'Why, Jack! What *do* you mean? Do I ever ask about your correspondence? Do please acquit me of *that* inquisitiveness!'

'Idiot! Of course not! But all the same, there's a piece of news come that will interest you, I think.'

'News that will interest me? Oh, Jack! Do you mean there's news of Gertrude's mother?'

'Not so far as I know. I wish there were. No; this is quite personal to you.'

Joey knit her brows. 'More pupils for the School, then?'

'There *are* two more coming next term. But that isn't it.'

'Two more? That will make five. And it's only our second term here! We shall soon grow out of Sarres. But if it isn't Frau Becker or the School, what can it be, then?'

By this time they had reached the door, so Jack merely opened it for her, and followed her into the big, square hall. There they were met by Miss Wilson, who made no effort to hide her excitement when she saw them, but forgot her snowy crown and her thirty-three years, and, as Jo said later on, rushed at them like a hungry cat after liver.

'Have you heard? Do you know?' she cried. 'Oh, isn't it wonderful?'

'Heard what? Know what? demanded Joey. 'What on earth is up with you, Nell?'

'Bill' paused. 'Is that my goddaughter? Oh, Joey! There's such a surprise waiting for you in the study! It came late last night.' She turned to Dr Maynard. 'Did you get Hilda's message?'

'Yes; it came this morning with the post. But I've told Jo nothing about it yet. That's why she's all at sea and thinking you've gone off at half-cock.—Cheer up, Joey! Nell's quite sane, though I admit she doesn't look like it.—Here; take the kids, Nell, and we'll go to the study.'

'Oh, shove them down over there by the fire,' said Miss Wilson surprisingly, for she adored them all, and her little goddaughter in particular. 'I'm coming to see the fun.'

'I wish I knew what was the matter with you people!'

complained Jo as she superintended the parking of her daughters in a safe place.

The next moment there came a rush and a scurry of hard, padded feet and a mass of gold and brown and white flung himself on her, baying loudly.

'Rufus!' cried Jo, going down on her knees, her arms round a big neck, her face buried in the thick ruff of a magnificent St Bernard. 'Oh, my precious Rufus! Where have you come from? I thought I'd lost you for ever!'

'Actually,' said Jack, smiling down at his wife, 'he has just come from quarantine. He was brought over to England six months ago—in a very bad state, poor fellow, which is why you weren't told—and the quarantine authorities have done their best by him. He's in very different shape from what he was when I last saw him.'

'Oh, Jack! You don't know how miserable I've been about him!' And Jo hugged Rufus again, while he made valiant efforts at washing her face with his big tongue, and did succeed in beating a flail-like tail over her shoulders.

Jack said nothing. More than ever he was thankful that Jo had not seen her pet as he had been when he reached England—emaciated, covered with bruises and cuts, and with his magnificent coat a dirty, bedraggled mat. Rufus was still thin, but he looked almost like himself. He had been brought by poor Jockel, a half-wit who had been employed about the grounds of the Chalet School at the Tiern See. Jockel had had as bad a time as his charge, and had contrived to get away, no one knew how. He had adored Joey, and knowing her love for the great dog, which she had rescued as a fortnight-old puppy from drowning when she herself was a wild schoolgirl of fourteen, had contrived to get him. The two had wandered through western Europe, and had finally reached Bordeaux, where Jockel had fallen in with Cornelia Flower's father. That understanding gentleman had engaged the lad as a servant, and sent Rufus over to England. Now, here he was, wagging his tail, and looking up with pathetic golden-brown eyes into the face of Dr Jack, to whom he owed many good walks and frolics in the old days when Jo, at school, had been unable to have him with her.

In the excitement Jo almost forgot what her husband and Nell Wilson had been talking about, and cried joyfully all over the St Bernard, until Jack, thinking this was enough, roused her by remarking casually, 'Don't you want to know how he was brought over to Guernsey?'

Jo got to her feet, dashing the tears from her eyes with the back of her hand. 'Of course I do! How *did* you manage it? There's no boat for two or three days at this time of year.'

'He was flown across,' said her husband.

'*Flown* across? Who by?'

'What appalling grammar! By an old friend who was bringing two other old friends. They're waiting for us in the study, I gather. Shall we go along and welcome them?'

'Old friends? The Lannises? Mr Flower?' Joey was still caressing Rufus's head, and he was leaning against her, looking up into her eyes with all the adoration of his soul. In quarantine he had received kindness. His hungry stomach had been filled; his cuts and bruises tended; his coat treated till it shone with the same gloss it had known in the happy days at the Tiern See and the Sonnalpe. But Rufus had always longed for his mistress. Now he had her, and it would be strange if anyone could part them again.

Jack grinned as he replied, 'No, my child. You're very wide of the mark. Come along and see.'

Casting a glance at her daughters who had slumbered placidly through most of this, Joey meekly followed him along the passage to the room which had been turned over to Miss Annersley for a study, Rufus clinging to her side. Miss Wilson followed them, her eyes alight with interest. The bell between lessons had rung three minutes ago, and she was due in the Sixth for a geography lesson; but she left the lesson and the Sixth, to take care of themselves, determined to see Jo's reaction to the latest excitement. Hurrying along the corridor from the Fourth, where she had been giving a lesson on English grammar, came Miss Annersley; and Simone Lecoutier abandoned the Fifth and algebraic progression and shot after them like a schoolgirl, her eyes gleaming, and her lips parted in a wide smile, a flush on her usually sallow cheeks. So it was quite a little procession that halted outside of the closed door when Joey stretched out her free hand—the other still rested on Rufus's head—and turned the handle.

There was a little rustle within, of someone springing up. Then Jo opened the door to meet the full blaze of December sunlight dazzling her eyes after the dark passage. She took an uncertain step or two forward, and heard a joyful cry of 'Joey—oh, Joey liebchen!'

For a moment Joey stood in stunned amazement. Then she leapt forward. An ecstatic cry of *'Frieda!'* broke from her lips as she saw a slight fair girl, with apple-blossom colouring and the blue eyes of her north Tyrolean ancestry. The next moment the two friends, so long parted, were in each other's arms, mingling tears, while the rest stood round regarding them with satisfaction.

'Oh, Frieda!' gasped Jo, as always, the first to recover herself. 'Where *have* you come from? How did you get here? Are you going to stay? Oh!' with sudden recollection, 'was it you who brought my Rufus? You couldn't have done anything dearer to me! Thank you more than I can say!'

Frieda laughed, and dried her eyes. 'Joey, if that were all—but see who else has come with me!'

Joey wheeled round to see two young men standing regarding her with smiles. For one moment she stared unbelievingly. Then, as her husband told her with mock severity later on, she threw all decorum to the winds, and, freeing herself from Frieda's hold, rushed on first one and then the other, embracing them rapturously.

'Friedel! And Bruno!' she cried. 'Safe—safe! And we feared you were both dead! Oh, how wonderful it all is!'

Friedel von Glück and Bruno von Ahlen returned her

embraces, and then Rufus, evidently feeling left out in the cold, bayed loudly, and promptly came from the hall the angry cries of babies rudely wakened from sleep.

'The babes!' cried Jo. 'Wait, everyone! I simply must show you at once! I hope no one's given the show away!' This last was shouted back over her shoulder as she fled to her daughters' rescue.

The three newcomers swung round on Jack Maynard, who, having kissed Frieda, and wrung the hands of the other two men, was standing with a twinkle in his eyes.

Frieda grabbed Jack Maynard's arm. 'Jack! Have you and Joey a baby?—No; but she said "babes!" Twins, then, like Peggy and Rix! Oh, why did no one tell me! How old are they? Are they boys or girls or one of each? When did they—' The last word died unspoken on her lips, for at that moment Joey entered the room, proudly bearing a basketful of indignant babies, who all yelled together at the full pitch of excellent lungs.

Frieda sped across the floor to help her friend. Then she stopped, staring at the babies with incredulous eyes. Friedel and Bruno stepped forward to see what had startled her. The next moment they, too, were staring with dropped jaws, as Joey carefully laid the basket down on the table, and proceeded to extract her eldest daughter, whom she presented to Miss Wilson.

'Take your goddaughter, Nell. Jack, here's Connie for you. And this is my baby, Margot. Triplets, Frieda! Can you beat it?'

The babies were hushed, and shown off, and Frieda kneeling down by the chair in which Jo had ensconced herself with little Margot, exclaimed at the vividly blue eyes; the thick thatch of red hair, already wavy, though none of the triplets could show the curls that adorned their young cousins; and the beautiful pink and white complexion.

'Joey! What lovely babies! Triplets! Oh, how like you!' And Frieda rocked with laughter.

'That's what everyone says,' returned Jo. 'I don't see why.'

'Oh, you always did do things *thoroughly*. But surely you've overstepped the mark this time! Oh, aren't they little flowers, Bruno?'

She lifted her eyes to Bruno von Ahlen's face, and he smiled as he laid a hand on her golden head with its coronal of heavy plaits.

'They are beautiful babies, Jo. And, as Frieda says, little flowers. What are their names, and which is the oldest?'

Joey explained, and when the babies had been soothed, Frieda sat down and held out her arms. 'Let me nurse the three at once. I've never held triplets before. Oh, Joey! What a surprise for everyone.'

But Joey paid no heed to this. Her quick eyes had spied the gleam of gold on her friend's finger. Swiftly, she caught at Bruno von Ahlen's left hand, and inspected the wedding-ring thereon.

'When were you two married?—Yes; take the babes, Frieda, if you want them. Mind, Len is an awful wriggler! Hold her tight! And how did you escape. Does Wanda know yet? Oh, what a joyful Christmas this will be!'

Presently, when Miss Wilson and Simone had been recalled to a sense of their duties, and the babies were sleeping peacefully again in their basket, they all sat down, Rufus as close to Jo as he could be, and Bruno von Ahlen and Friedel von Glück told her the story of their past eighteen months. Not that they told her all, or even a fifth of it. Much was not fit to be repeated. Some they told to Jack Maynard later on. Jo could see that both must have suffered. Friedel's thick black hair showed streaks of grey. Bruno's face was lined and haggard. Even Frieda looked older than her years warranted, with all she had undergone during the period. But all were very happy, and all rejoiced that they had escaped from the horrors of Nazidom to the freedom of England.

Both young men had been in one concentration camp, though both refused to say much about it. They had endured tortures, and had known cold and semi-starvation for months. Knocked about and brutally beaten for the slightest offence, the wonder was that they had survived. Then, when the famous purge of the end of October had taken place, they had contrived to escape, thanks to the help of three men whose names they flatly refused to give.

'Oh, why not?' cried Joey. 'I wanted to pray for them, seeing it's the one thing I *can* do in the circumstances.'

'Safer not,' said Friedel curtly. Then he went on. 'We got away by Untergrundbahn—no; not a *real* railway, Joey. Don't be so silly! That is just what we called it. We went to Turin, where Bruno and Frieda became engaged. Then we got Herr Mensch and Kurt to agree to come to England with us. So long as they were there, if Hitler chose to order them back to the Reich as he has ordered the Baltic Germans, there was danger that they might have to go.'

'What! Are Onkel Reise and Tante Gretchen here as well?' demanded Joey. 'And Bernhilda and Kurt, are *they* here, too?'

'Not in Guernsey. They have gone to Gisela and Gottfried. But they hope to come soon. Meanwhile,' went on Friedel, 'Bruno and Frieda were married—very quietly. And we chartered a plane, and called at quarantine for Rufus whom Jockel told me was in England—oh, yes; we met Mr Flower in Bordeaux, and saw Jockel, poor lad! —We got here last night, and I went straight to Wanda. Bruno and Frieda came here. He and I stay for a fortnight, and then we go to join the French Foreign Legion—if they will have us. If not, we will join the Polish Legion. Mercifully, I have Polish blood in my veins, and his grandmother was a Pole, so we shall be eligible. Now you know the whole story.'

'One last thing, Joey,' said Bruno. 'I want you to have Frieda to live with you while I am away. Will you?'

'Oh, *willen't* I?' cried Jo, throwing an arm round her friend. 'I ask nothing better. You'll come, won't you, Frieda?'

Frieda gave a tearful smile. 'I should like it above all things.'

There was a moment's silence. Then Jo lifted a sparkling face to ask, 'Do the School know that they've come?'

'No, Joey. They were all so tired that when Frieda and her husband arrived, we packed them off to bed, and as it was late, the girls were already asleep. Then, this morning, we didn't have them called. In fact, they'd just finished breakfast when Friedel came over from Wanda,' said Miss Annersley. 'You are the first after ourselves to know of it.'

'Oh, then, as it's nearly time for Break, couldn't you stop lessons for once, and let the girls see them all?' pleaded Joey. 'Rufus, too. Rob and Daisy will be thrilled about him. They've missed him horribly.'

'What appalling things you do suggest, Joey!' cried shy Frieda.

'My dear, if you say one more word, I'll—I'll make them all dance a wedding ring round you as we did Bernie at her wedding,' declared Jo, taking her babies from Frieda, and returning them to their basket.

'Anyone would think those children of yours were puppies or kittens, you treat them so casually,' said Friedel with a chuckle.

'That's put on for your especial benefit,' declared 'Bill.' 'She's as proud as a peacock with two tails, really, to think she's beaten Marie and Wanda, and levelled up with her sister.'

'Nell! Of all the mean things to say! And I *don't* treat them casually, either!' cried outraged Jo. 'They're as comfy as possible! Just look at them, Frieda! Aren't they snug?'

Frieda came laughing, and slipped an arm round Jo's waist as they bent over the babies. 'They've lovely red hair, Jo. It's redder than Sybil's, isn't it? Hers is chestnut. These people are a really copper red. Didn't Mrs Bettany say her youngest girl has red hair?'

'Maeve? Yes—but it's chestnut, like Sybil's. All right; I'm ready now, everyone.'

187

There came a tap at the door, and Biddy O'Ryan entered, followed by Elizabeth Arnett, both looking very sheepish. At sight of the visitors, the expression faded from Biddy's face. She gave vent to a loud yell of horror, and sprang for 'Bill,' clutching her round the waist, and burying her face against that startled lady's blouse.

'It's ghosts—'tis ghosts oi'm seeing!'

'Bill' shook herself free with vigour. 'Stop, Biddy, you stupid child! Ghosts, indeed! What have you been reading lately? It's only Herr von Glück and Dr von Ahlen come safely back.—Oh, and Frieda, who is his wife now,' she added.

Biddy opened the eyes she had screwed up tightly, and stared at the trio with open mouth. ''Tis yourselves,' she said dramatically. Then with a bound she was at the door. 'And 'tis meself will tell the rest.' And she was gone before anyone could stop her.

'Wait, Elizabeth!' said Miss Annersley peremptorily, just as that young person was about to sidle out after her companion. 'Why were you sent?'

'We—we were making a noise—rather—' stammered Elizabeth. 'Yvette came, and—and—well, perhaps we *were* rather rude. Anyhow, she sent us to report ourselves to you. I'm sorry, Miss Annersley.'

Her words were interrupted by loud cheers, and then flying feet came scampering down the passage. The Fourth, the Fifth, and the Sixth were taking advantage of the fact that no mistresses were with them, and were coming to greet the long-lost wanderers, while the other forms, hearing the noise and under the impression that an air-raid practice must be in progress, though they had missed the warning, poured out of the form-rooms after them. So Joey had her way, and Friedel, and Frieda, and Bruno were welcomed in style, if somewhat cramped style, by the Chalet School. Finally, Miss Annersley, taking pity on them all, swept the whole party, including Rufus, into Hall, where the visitors were marched to the dais, and a speech demanded from them.

Springing forward—who would have thought of shy

188

Frieda doing it?—she cried, 'I'll tell you something, girls —something to make you prouder than ever of belonging to the Chalet School. When Bruno and Friedel were helped to escape, one of the men who helped them told them that his sister had been at the School and was a member of the Chalet School Peace League. He said that what she had told him of our aims had made him ashamed of many of the things they were driven to do— especially as she was in prison because she would tell none of the Chalet School secrets—and she is only nine-teen—younger than Joey and I are. If it hadn't been for her, Bruno and Friedel might have died in concentra-tion camp. But *because* of her, they are safe with us today. They are going back to France, to fight for the Allies. It may be that neither will ever come back. But Wanda and I both feel that we owe their lives to our School, and we are proud—*proud*—PROUD of belong-ing to such a School!' Then she broke down and cried, and the girls, with lumps in their throats, sang, 'For she's a jolly good fellow.'

'And so it's all come from our League,' said Joey that night as she and Jack sat together in their pretty drawing-room.

'Yes; and talking of your League,' he fumbled in a pocket and produced a sealed and sadly begrimed envelope, 'you as one of the signatories of the said League, might now like to take charge of the document itself. It was found on the Robin's very exhausted little person that night when Gottfried brought her home and we nearly died of fright looking for her.'

Joey gulped and stared. 'But, Jack! Wherever?—How did—?'

Jack placed the envelope in his wife's hands, which he held close in his, while he explained. 'There isn't much to tell,' he said quietly. 'I smuggled it out of Austria— along with my own precious belongings,' he gave a meaning glance into Joey's eyes. 'I kept it safe in hiding ever since, with the express purpose of producing it again on a suitable occasion. It seems to me that this is a most suitable occasion.'

Joey's heart and mind were too full for speaking, for through this travel-stained relic she seemed to see the Sonnalpe with its magic carpet of flowers, snow-clad mountains pink and purple in the glow of the evening sun, and the Tiern See alive with dancing shadows. Her thoughts became audible: '*Olim meminisse juvabit,*' she quoted.

'I beg your pardon, dear?' Jack's mystified question brought Joey back to earth.

'Sorry, old boy,' she said with a penitent smile, 'What a brick you've been! How thrilled Robin and the others will be tomorrow when they hear of the later history of our League Covenant.'

'Yes,' said Jack. 'It might seem a very small thing—the peace effort of a lot of schoolgirls. But that effort has meant the lives of two fine fellows, and Frieda's happiness. God bless the Chalet School Peace League, say I!'

'So do I,' said Joey. 'And even when peace comes, the League must continue.'

'Woof! I quite agree!' barked Rufus; and so had the last word.